DEKOK AND THE SORROWING TOMCAT

DeKok
and the
Sorrowing Tomcat

by

BAANTJER

translated from the Dutch by H.G. Smittenaar

INTERCONTINENTAL PUBLISHING

ISBN 1 881164 61 6

Printing History:
>1st Dutch printing: 1974
>2nd Dutch printing: October, 1978
>3rd Dutch printing: December, 1979
>4th Dutch printing: January, 1982
>5th Dutch printing: November, 1984
>6th Dutch printing: May, 1986
>7th Dutch printing: October, 1988
>8th Dutch printing: August, 1990
>9th Dutch printing: April, 1991
>10th Dutch printing: May, 1991
>11th Dutch printing: August, 1991
>12th Dutch printing: September, 1992
>13th Dutch printing: March, 1993

A condensed version of this book appeared in the original language in *Het Beste boek* (Best Books), a publication of Uitgeversmaatschappij The Reader's Digest. Copyright 1981 by Uitgeversmaatschappij The Reader's Digest N.V., Amsterdam & Brussels.

>1st American edition: May, 1993
>Hardcover edition: June, 1993

Also published as soft-cover edition under ISBN 1-881164-05-5

Typography: Monica S. Rozier
Cover Painting: Judy Sardella, adapted from the series
    Studies of a black cat by Judy Sardella.
Manufactured by BookCrafters, Inc., Fredericksburg, VA

DeKok
and the
Sorrowing Tomcat

1

Peter Geffel, commonly known as "Cunning Pete" had to come to a bad end. Even his own mother had predicted that many times. He died at a youthful age. It was a quick and violent death.

It happened during the winter in the deserted sand dunes along the coast near Seadike. The sand dunes, in addition to the many dikes, protect the low countries of the Netherlands from flooding. In times gone by it used to be the *only* protection for a country that is largely below sea level. Because of their importance to the ecology, to protect the sparse vegetation and the overall security of the nation, access is restricted in many places and one is never allowed to stray from the established paths. In summer the paths are crowded with people going to the beach, but in winter the landscape is desolate and resembles a desert.

And there Pete Geffel was found by a lonely jogger. On the path, just before it split into two directions. Cunning Pete was prone, both arms outstretched, the long, slender fingers half buried in the loose sand and a narrow dagger in his back. The Seadike police, a total force of less than twenty officers, immediately cordoned off the scene of the crime and with assistance from the State Police carefully went over the ground.

The result was far from hopeful. There were no clear signs. Dogs, brought in for the purpose of sniffing out any possible scents, were no help. Bred and trained primarily for city situations in the most densely populated country in the world, some were too excited by the traces of rabbits all around and one remained at the fork in the path, loudly barking at a number of tire tracks. About three hundred yards down the path was a well-kept paved road that led to the rest of the Netherlands and from there to more than 300 million Dutch, Belgians, Germans, French, Italians and other members of the EEC.

The chief of the Seadike police, close to retirement, decided after a few hours that there were no obvious clues, that the list of suspects could very well include any of the millions of Europeans and that there was no credit to be gained for his department in the case of the murdered Pete Geffel. He withdrew to his headquarters, a comfortable bungalow near the beach, and issued an All Points Bulletin. Then he had another cup of coffee and decided to wait for results.

* * *

Hands deep in his trouser pockets and with a face like a thundercloud, Detective-Inspector DeKok of the Amsterdam Municipal Police (Homicide) paced up and down the large, cheerless detective room in the old, renowned police station at 48 Warmoes Street.

The building had been a police station as long as anybody could remember. There were those who speculated that it could have served as such for Rembrandt's

"Nightwatch". The "Nightwatch", Rembrandt's largest and possibly most famous painting, was completed in 1642. The original title of the painting was "The Company of Captain Frans Banning Cocq". Captain Cocq was the head of the local constabulary at the time. More than 300 years ago, his men roamed the same streets, alleys and canals that were currently patrolled by the men and women of the Warmoes Street Station. Even then the area was known as a "Red Light District".

The current building was most certainly old and its interior could have served as a set for "Hill Street Blues". Some did indeed refer to it as the Dutch Hill Street. Among police officers, it was generally known as the busiest police station in Europe, situated as it was on the edge of Amsterdam's Red Light District and hemmed in by the harbor and a polyglot population encompassing all strata of society, from aristocrats to day-laborers and from drug dealers to respectable business people. A hundred or more languages could be heard in the Quarter, churches could be found cheek-to-jowl with brothels and the bars never closed.

As he paced up and down, DeKok reflected on the many hours he had spent this way. He had been on the force for more than twenty years and the last fifteen as a plain-clothed policeman. Sometimes he thought with fondness of his early days as a street cop, a constable in uniform, whose only responsibility was to be turned out neatly and on time. To patrol the assigned beat and to represent the Law. Reports were seldom made in those days. The cop on the beat administered justice, settled disputes and watched over his neighborhood with a fatherly indulgence. In many ways it had been a good life. There were few violent crimes. Amsterdam did not even have a specific Homicide department in those days. Murders were so rare.

Now it was different. As everywhere else in the world, crime had increased in Amsterdam as well. And the crimes had become more violent. Gone were the "good old days". Gone forever. Police work had become more technical, more detail-oriented. It seemed to DeKok that reports and red tape were becoming increasingly more important than keeping the peace, more significant than tangible results. It went against his nature. DeKok was an old-fashioned cop, a "hands-on" policeman.

He knew there was an assortment of files in the drawer of his desk. Files from cases that should get his attention, that needed to be addressed. But DeKok ignored them. He could not be bothered with routine just now, or for the past several days, for that matter. A strange unrest plagued him. It was as if a disturbing, outside influence, like static on the radio, interfered with the sensitive nerve endings in his brain creating a sensation of unrest, of expectation. Subconsciously he was waiting for something grand, something wild, something unusual, something that would require all his knowledge and ingenuity. It made him restless and it made him irritable. That is why he cursed. He cursed everything: the wet snow that covered the streets like a dirty, cold, sticky porridge, the Commissaris,* his immediate boss, because he had urged DeKok several times to complete his ongoing cases and he cursed his invaluable assistant, Vledder, because there was nothing but dregs left in the coffee pot.

Dick Vledder allowed his fingers to rest lightly on the keys of his computer terminal and looked at DeKok with a worried face. Not for the first time he reflected on the similarity between the names of DeKok and that of Captain Cocq and thought about how well DeKok would have fitted

---

* Commissaris = a rank equivalent to Captain.

in that time. He noticed the discontent in his partner, mentor and friend and he knew that the curses were not aimed at him, or anybody, or anything in particular. They were used as a release. At times, DeKok seemed to have an uncanny feeling for what was going to happen. A sort of precognition. He knew *something* was about to happen, he just did not know *what* was going to happen.

Most of the time DeKok was an amiable person with an even, kind disposition. But Vledder had seen him in this mood before. He had witnessed the dark side of DeKok's character several times. Always it had been a prelude, a prologue to murder, to mystery.

Vledder wondered what sort of difficulties were brewing in the thunderclouds on the horizon of DeKok's premonition. One never knew, with DeKok. He had a way to get involved in the most bizarre and impossible situations, almost in the blinking of an eye. Young Vledder thought about the many cases they had worked on together, the situations in which they had been involved, the characters they had met. He grinned ruefully to himself. Slowly he stood up and walked over to the window. A small measure of DeKok's uneasiness had sparked a similar disquiet in the young Inspector.

Outside, the wet snow kept coming down.

* * *

Gus Shenk entered the detective room and distributed copies of a number of telex messages. Although most of the old telex machines had long since been replaced by modern fax machines, almost everybody still stubbornly referred to them as "telexes".

Gus was a former beat-cop. Once, when pursuing a burglar over the quaint rooftops of Amsterdam, he slipped and fell thirty feet to the ground. It had done something to his back and he was declared to be unfit for active duty. Since that time he had been in charge of communications at Warmoes Street. But it rankled. In his heart he was still a beat-cop, wishing he was back, pounding the pavement along the canals of Amsterdam.

He had been in communications for years and his special interest were the fax messages, or, as Gus too, insisted on calling them, the telexes. The detective branch appreciated Shenk's interest. Because of his long experience in the streets, he was able to separate the really important messages from the merely routine and he often added his own, sometimes sharp, but always knowledgeable notes to the incoming information.

He walked over to DeKok, one leg dragging, and pushed a message form into his hands.

"Hey, DeKok, isn't Pete Geffel an old customer of yours as well? I seem to remember that you once sent him up. Embezzlement, or something like that. At least, that's what I seem to remember."

DeKok read the telex from Seadike. His eyebrows rippled. The wrinkles in his forehead deepened.

"When did this come in?"

Shenk looked at him in surprise.

"Just now," he answered, aggrieved, "less than five minutes ago. Surely you don't think I would sit on something like this, do you?"

DeKok produced a smile. It was as if the sun had come through the thunderclouds. He placed a brotherly arm on Shenk's shoulder.

"It was a stupid question, Gus," he answered pleasant-ly. "A real stupid question. Of course you didn't sit on it. Especially not a message about Pete Geffel. After all, it's no secret, the whole force knows you always had a weak spot for that guy."

Gus Shenk shrugged his shoulders reluctantly, as if wanting to deny the statement.

"A weak spot," he growled, "what do you call a weak spot? In the old days, maybe, when he wasn't even a teenager yet, yes, when his actions were little more than pranks, yes, maybe I had a weak spot for him *then*. I sure liked him, *then*. Although I've had to chase him a number of times." He paused and smiled at the memory. "Strange really, no matter what he did, I could really never get angry with the kid. I mean, really angry. Of course I pretended. He started to lie the moment I laid hands on him. Goodness, how that boy could lie! It was incredible! You wondered where he got it from. He lied with a straight face, daring you to disbelieve him. As I saw it, it was just a game for him. He just loved to play pranks, to fool people." He shook his head somberly. "Too bad," he sighed, "that he later used his talents to make a dishonest living."

DeKok made a vague gesture.

"Not everybody's like you, Gus. There's plenty of people who don't like being lied to, being made a fool of. I think Pete finally met somebody who didn't take his lies as a joke, a game, but somebody who took revenge."

Shenk looked at him.

"That must have been it," he said slowly. "You're right, that must have been it." He stared at the message in DeKok's hands.

13

"Dumb kid . . ." He sounded sad. For another moment he stood there, deep in thought. Then he turned abruptly and walked out of the room.

DeKok stared after him in silence. He knew so well what was going on in old Shenk's mind. He was familiar with the feeling from his own experience. A cop would always meet petty criminals, or even big criminals, who, for one reason or another, struck a sympathetic cord, despite their contempt for the Law. It was almost inevitable. If one liked people, and most police officers did, it came with the job. It was simply impossible to always maintain a strict official, distant attitude.

DeKok thoughtfully chewed his lower lip. He felt sorry for Shenk, who had been so suddenly confronted with the murder of his former protege, without warning, via a fax message. And suddenly he felt a resentment, a deep resentment against the man, or woman, who had killed Pete Geffel in the deserted sand dunes near Seadike, who had plunged a dagger in the back of "Cunning" Pete. Regardless of the motives, that could never be justified. DeKok had a personal, as well as a professional abhorrence of murder. To him murder with a knife, or a dagger, was twice as repellent.

He ambled over to the coat rack, slipped into his old raincoat and placed his small, decrepit felt hat on his head.

Vledder approached.

"Where are you going?"

DeKok did not answer. He could ignore people and things with a sublime indifference when it suited him. It was one of his most endearing, or irritating, habits, depending on the situation, or one's point of view. He finished buttoning his coat and handed the message to Vledder.

"Look in the files and see what you can find out about the victim. We must have quite a bit on him. He's an old customer. Be sure to check nicknames."

"Nicknames?"

"Yes, you'll find him listed under 'Cunning' Pete."

Vledder nodded.

"And what about you?"

"What *do* you mean?"

"Where are you going?"

DeKok pushed his hat further back on his head and rubbed his face with a flat hand.

"I'm going to see Little Lowee. I want to know when was the last time Pete had a beer, there."

* * *

Louis, nicknamed "Little Lowee", because of his negligible size, was well known in the Red Light District and was an old acquaintance of Detective-Inspector DeKok. For years, almost since the beginning of his police career, DeKok had been a frequent visitor in the narrow, intimate little bar of Little Lowee at the corner of Barn Alley. Over the exquisite aroma of fine, old cognac, sipped over the years, a strange sort of friendship had gradually grown between the two men. It was a relationship that was strictly regulated by the limitations imposed by the Law. Yet, the two men, so different in background and outlook on life, genuinely seemed to like each other. But somewhere within the vague concepts of Law and Order they would always be on opposite sides. After all, DeKok represented the Law. And that sort of people, according to Lowee's tolerant reasoning, had some peculiar ideas about what was right and what was wrong. One had to make allowances for that. But it did not

15

hamper the friendship, thought Lowee, unless you let it. You just had to take it into account.

* * *

DeKok shook the snow from his hat in the minuscule lobby and loosened his coat. Then he pushed the heavy, leather-bordered curtains out of his way and looked inside. It was quiet in the bar.

He ambled over to the end of the long bar and hoisted himself onto a stool. Little Lowee came over to his side, a friendly smile on his narrow face.

"Good morning, Mr. DeKok. Good to see you again. The same recipe?" Without waiting for an answer, he produced a bottle of Napoleon Cognac from under the counter and, almost in the same movement, placed two large snifters in front of DeKok and poured generous measures.

"Busy at Warmoes Street?"

"So, so," shrugged DeKok. "Can't complain. Always something going on. No recession in crime, ever."

"Well, consider it job security," laughed Little Lowee.

"To tell you the truth," sighed DeKok, "during the days before Christmas I don't feel much like it. I always feel that it should be a time to reflect, to take some interest in the people you have gotten to know in your job."

Lowee looked at him with one eye closed tightly.

"Remains to be seen, of course," allowed Lowee, "if them guys are all that happy about your interest."

DeKok ignored the remark.

"Sometimes," he said thoughtfully, "sometimes you can't help but wonder . . . What happened to them? How will they celebrate Christmas, this year?"

Lowee bounced restlessly on the balls of his feet.

16

"Geez, you're being downright gooey," he said, irritated. "Hey, DeKok, it's only your first drink, you know. I means, too soon to go all sentimental on me."

DeKok shook his head sadly, rocked the cognac in his glass and sighed again.

"No, really," he began hesitatingly. "For instance, take Cunning Pete, he was always such a jolly, cheerful guy. I wonder what happened to him. I haven't seen him for ages." He paused for a moment and then looked over his glass at the small barkeeper. "What about you, Lowee, seen him lately?"

Lowee did not answer at once. A small, but noticeable tic developed on his cheek.

"No ... eh, ...no," He stuttered, "I ... eh, I ain't seen him for ages meself."

DeKok smiled.

"You're a bad liar, Lowee. I've noticed that before. It's a weak spot, you know."

Lowee blushed.

"Another one, Mr. DeKok?" he asked. DeKok nodded slowly. The fine cognac, especially reserved for him, gurgled aromatically into the glass. Meanwhile DeKok observed the normally so steady hand of Little Lowee and wondered why the barkeeper was lying.

"I ... eh, ... I would really be interested," DeKok spoke somberly, "if ... eh, if I could talk to Pete for a moment. It would save us a lot of trouble and work."

Lowee looked at him with surprise on his face.

"You're looking for him, then?"

"Who?"

"Pete, Cunning Pete, he's wanted?"

A bit shyly, or so it appeared, DeKok scratched the back of his neck. He thought he had been clear enough.

"No," he said, shaking his head, "no, we're not looking for him. He's not wanted. I mean, we never have to look for him again, no, never again. You see, we found him, this morning, dead . . . a dagger in his back."

Lowee's mouth fell open in utter astonishment.

"Pete . . . dead? But only yesterday . . ."

At that moment a uniformed constable stormed into the bar and approached DeKok with long, hurried steps.

"Vledder told me I would find you here. You are to report at once to the Commissaris. We just heard that an armored car was robbed."

2

Commissaris Buitendam, the tall, distinguished chief of the police station at Warmoes Street, frowned. His gray, bristly eyebrows contracted when DeKok entered his office, coattails flying, hat pushed back from his forehead, busily, self-importantly. It was, of course, a pose, a farce, no more than contrived posturing. The Commissaris knew and DeKok knew the Commissaris knew and the Commissaris knew DeKok knew. The Commissaris was well acquainted with DeKok's abhorrence of order and discipline. The often brilliant Detective-Inspector simply did not seem to fit in the rigid harness of official hierarchy. It was impossible to contain him with rules and regulations. The gray sleuth was too individualistic. It explained why he would never be promoted beyond his present rank. But his brilliance, his obvious suitability for the important aspects of police work, guaranteed his continued employment. Nevertheless, any outward sign that might indicate that DeKok was submitting to discipline, to official guidelines, seemed like a parody, a police comedy. There was, reflected the Commissaris, something Keystone-Cop-like about DeKok at such moments.

Therefore the Commissaris frowned. He had no hope of duplicating DeKok's amazing feats in that department. DeKok, without any effort, or even any conscious volition, seemed to be able to actually ripple his eyebrows. It was a sight that never ceased to fascinate Vledder, who had seen it more often than most. According to Vledder, and many others, DeKok's eyebrows were able to, and did, live a life of their own. But all the Commissaris could do, was frown.

"I'm sorry I took so long," apologized DeKok. "I was warming a stool over at Little Lowee's."

The Commissaris made no attempt to hide his surprise.

"Stool? Lowee?"

DeKok gave him a friendly grin.

"Little Lowee, yes. You must know him, certainly? He pours some of the best cognac in town."

The Commissaris moved in his chair, coughed discreetly. The frivolous subject of "Cognac-Lowee-Stool" was not to his liking. He composed his features into a serious expression.

"Listen, DeKok," he said in a somewhat pompous voice. "There was an armed robbery about half an hour ago. It happened on Stuyvesant Quay, near Toll House Point. An armored truck, belonging to Bent & Goossens, the transport company, has been robbed by three armed and masked men. A considerable amount of money is involved. Management at B&G estimates the loss at around three million."

DeKok whistled softly between his teeth.

"A nice bit of change."

The Commissaris sighed.

"Indeed, a considerable sum. That value is in American dollars, by the way. Almost double that amount in guilders. The shipment consisted of banknotes from different countries. In that case the dollar value is used for convenience. A large sum, anyway. Probably a record for our little country. Therefore we can count on a considerable amount of publicity. You understand ... press, radio, television ..." He paused and looked at DeKok with a penetrating look. "That's why I want you to handle the case," he added.

DeKok made a deprecatory gesture.

"Not me. Please, no, I'd rather not, I mean. There must be others. Corstant, for instance, or Sweet and young Bonmeyer. I had other plans."

Buitendam's mouth fell open. He looked at DeKok in astonishment.

"Other plans?" he managed to ask.

DeKok nodded complacently.

"Yes, I thought I'd get involved in Pete Geffel's murder."

The Commissaris swallowed a sudden lump in his throat.

"You mean, the murder in Seadike. The one that came over the fax, earlier?"

DeKok nodded approvingly.

"Yes, that murder. Right."

Commissaris Buitendam rose abruptly from his chair. He did not like to be contradicted. It was something he simply could not, and would not, tolerate. It upset him considerably. His normally somewhat pale face became red with rage.

"You ... you!" he snarled. "You will concern yourself with the robbery on B&G. Nothing else. Understood? Get acquainted with the facts and make contact with the managing director, the president of the company, one Mr. Bent."

21

DeKok shrugged his shoulders in a hopeless gesture and walked toward the door. The Commissaris called him back.

"Team up with Vledder. He already has some of the details. The two of you had some success together, in the past. This time, too, I expect quick results."

DeKok hesitated for a moment, rubbed the bridge of his nose with a little finger.

"If," he began slowly, "... if I happen to encounter, purely by accident, of course ... if I happen to run into Pete Geffel's killer ..."

The Commissaris seemed on the verge of exploding.

"OUT!!!"

DeKok left.

* * *

Vledder laughed heartily.

"So, quarreling with the boss again, eh?"

DeKok grinned sadly.

"Well, yes," he said, irritated. "Why can't he let me be?" He chewed on his lower lip. "I used to have my differences with the old Commissaris, the previous one, I mean, but I was usually allowed to go my own way. But this one ..." He did not complete the sentence, bit his lower lip once more and then continued: "You see, Dick, it's a matter of sentiment, you know. Just like old Shenk, I remember Pete when he was a kid, they are good memories, despite his many pranks and, let's admit it, his many crimes. But he was a cheerful kid who developed into a happy-go-lucky man. I just don't like to think of him with a dagger in his back."

Vledder smiled in sympathy.

"You're taking it personally?"

DeKok nodded.

"Yes. What do I care about three million, or thirty million, or even three hundred million? Nothing, absolutely nothing at all, at all. Those guys at B&G just have to be a bit more careful with their money. Deep down I hope that the robbers get away with it." He grinned like a schoolboy. "In any case, far enough away so they'll be outside my jurisdiction."

Vledder looked at him with amazement.

"You mean that?"

DeKok shrugged his shoulders.

"Let's not get into it. Tell me what you know about the hold-up."

Vledder sighed.

"Not much. Probably no more than the Commissaris already told you. It happened on Stuyvesant Quay, near Toll House Point, behind the Central Railroad Station, the old one, that is. Two masked men, armed with pistols robbed an armored truck of Currency Transport, Incorporated."

DeKok looked up.

"Currency Transport, Incorporated? I thought the Commissaris mentioned B&G and he also mentioned *three* men."

Vledder nodded agreement.

"You're right. Currency Transport is a division of B&G. You know, they're into everything. If you want it moved, no matter what, they'll move it for you. Freight, household goods, money, you name it. They move it by truck, by barge, by plane, whatever. They're big!" He took a deep breath. "About the men," he continued, "two held up the truck and took the money. The third one was behind the wheel of a fast car, probably a Simca 1500, blue, or light blue."

"Stolen?"

"We don't know yet. You see, two Simcas were stolen last night, both Models 1500 and both were blue. One was stolen in Haarlem and the other from Heemstede, one of the suburbs of Haarlem. Most likely one of these cars was used during the hold-up. We don't know which one, at this time."

"Did anybody get the license tag?"

"Yes, NG 12-83."

"That's a very old number."

Vledder grinned.

"Right, a very old number. It used to belong to a Chevrolet. The Chevy was junked more than three years ago."

DeKok pushed his lower lip forward.

"Smart guys." There was admiration in his voice.

Vledder glanced at his notes.

"You can say that again. Smart guys. The entire hold-up shows professionalism. The timing was excellent. At exactly three minutes past ten, the truck stopped at the rear of the Railroad Station and the two guards in the back alighted with the money. The driver remained behind the wheel. The money was in a large crate, destined for shipment by rail. At that precise moment the Simca pulled up. Before anybody, least of all the guards, had any notion of what was happening, they were staring down the barrels of a couple of pistols and they were relieved of the crate. It all happened so quickly that nobody really noticed anything untoward." He flipped a page. "There was a constable on duty, not far away, and he didn't notice anything, either. He reacted immediately when one of the guards finally yelled at him. He shot at the fleeing car."

"Fired?" DeKok's eyebrows rippled dangerously. Despite the situation, Vledder paused briefly to be amazed at the sight. Then he answered:

24

"Yes, twice."

"Well?"

"Nothing. The Simca disappeared at a high rate of speed in the direction of the Harbor Building. But, according to the constable, he scored at least one hit. Shall I call him? His name is Bever, he's next door, writing his report."

DeKok nodded.

"Fetch him."

Constable Bever was an athletically built man in his middle thirties, with lively gestures and a playful mimicry. He showed a rueful grin when he took a seat across from DeKok.

"You can't help but wonder," began Constable Bever. "I mean, they steal three million right from under your nose. It's just plain shameful." He shook his head despondently. "How will I ever explain *that* to my son?"

DeKok grinned back at him

"I don't know, I am not your son," he said. "My name is DeKok, with . . . eh, kay-oh-kay. Much to my regret I'm in charge of this case. I heard you shot at the fleeing car. What do you think? You think you hit something, or somebody?"

Bever spread both arms wide.

"Well, I'm a good shot, DeKok. Most certainly. I'm usually in the top three during the shooting competitions. But, well, the car was a good distance away and rapidly disappearing when I first heard the yelling of the guards. They were pointing at the car. I fired twice. I aimed for the left rear tire. From where I was standing that was the easiest shot. But I missed. There was a slight deviation and both bullets hit the edge of the trunk." He made a dejected gesture. "It was no use trying a third shot. By then the car was too far away."

25

DeKok nodded silently.

"Would it be possible that you hit one of the occupants?"

Bever shrugged.

"Hard to say. I don't think so." He paused, hesitated. "To be honest, I hope not. I mean, you've got to admit it, DeKok, that was a professional piece of work. Nobody got hurt during the hold-up. It was fast, silent and almost unnoticed. I mean, I was barely fifty feet away and I didn't notice anything until the guards started to yell. I saw the truck stop, of course I did, but ..." He paused, gripped his head with both hands in a hopeless gesture. "I should be let go, it's simply too much. A robbery with a haul of three million and I'm practically watching it without doing anything about it." Bever groaned, his eyes closed.

DeKok looked at him.

"How long have you been on the force?"

"Five years."

"Well, then you should know that this sort of thing can happen. I wouldn't worry too much about it." DeKok waved negligently. "Return to your report. And if the Commissaris, or your sergeant, if either speaks harshly to you, just let it roll off. Be like a duck."

"A duck?"

"Yes, water rolls off a duck's back, let the reprimands roll off yours."

Shaking his head, Constable Bever left the room. It was a black day in his career, he thought, no matter what DeKok said.

When the constable had left, DeKok rose from his chair and started to pace up and down the large room. He invariably did that when he wanted to think. The cadence of his ambling gait helped to organize his thoughts. After a while he stopped in front of Vledder's desk.

"If I remember correctly," he said thoughtfully, "B&G has been in business for some time."

Vledder nodded.

"Oh, yes, at least three generations and more than twenty years in the armored car business, that is CTI, the division, was formed more than twenty years ago."

"And this is their first hold-up?"

"Yes, it has never happened before. Perhaps it lulled them into a false sense of security. They became more lax, perhaps, without really noticing it."

DeKok rubbed his chin pensively.

"Are the transports always for such large amounts? I mean, three million seems a lot, doesn't it?"

Vledder nodded.

"Yes it is," he answered. "But it's usually not that much. Their main business is transport between banks, you see. The average amount on a truck is usually between four and five hundred thousand. The rest is checks and papers. This time the amount of cash was extremely high. The robbers were lucky."

DeKok grinned. It transformed his craggy face into that of a mischievous schoolboy. Few people could resist a grinning DeKok.

"Sometimes," he said mysteriously, "sometimes Lady Luck receives a helping hand."

Vledder looked at him, wondering.

"What *do* you mean?"

DeKok shrugged.

"Just exactly what I'm saying. Sometimes Lady Luck gets a helping hand. B&G has been transporting money for more than twenty years. For twenty years one transport follows another, one run after another, without incidents. Nothing happens. Don't you think it's rather coincidental that suddenly, the one time they carry a larger than usual amount of cash, they're robbed? A bit too convenient, don't you think?"

Vledder came from behind his desk in a highly agitated state of mind. His round, somewhat boyish face showed he was excited.

"Why?" he questioned loudly, "Why should it be too much of a coincidence. It's possible, after all. I interrogated the guards thoroughly, I can assure you. There's no question of complicity. They're completely innocent."

DeKok looked at Vledder for long moments. Then he smiled.

"Come on, Dick," he said amicably, "get your coat. We have an appointment with Mr. Bent."

3

DeKok and Vledder were standing in the enormous hall of the B&G building. A bit lost, they looked around.

A large, tall black granite column rose up in the middle of the hall, supporting an enormous, bronze bust of the late Mr. Josephus Johannes Maria Goossens, the co-founder of the Company. He had died childless. The current Bent was the third President of Bent & Goossens by that name. On either side of the statue, wide marble staircases wended upstairs in a curve before meeting at an elaborate balcony overlooking the hall. Glistening crystal chandeliers hung from the high ceiling and the walls reflected the light from expensive marble. It was very beautiful and impressive.

DeKok pressed his lips together.

Interiors that were aimed at impressing visitors, had exactly the opposite effect on DeKok. He would not be impressed, or awed, or influenced by it. It only aroused in him feelings of inexplicable rebellion. Part, if not most, of that was caused by the puritanical soul of the civil servant and his Calvinistic childhood.

He took another look around and felt the dissatisfaction and discontent grow within him.

A neatly dressed gentleman in a dark suit caught the attention of the two police inspectors. From a glass booth he moved a crooked index finger in a beckoning gesture.

DeKok had a long standing dislike of beckoning gentlemen in glass booths. Therefore he did not make any effort to obey the beckoning finger, but instead beckoned back with his own crooked index finger. He smiled pleasantly and persisted in that attitude until the authoritarian gentlemen left his cage, dark red with rage.

"You are supposed to report to me." The man's voice was excited.

DeKok's eyebrows performed one of their famous dances. For once the effect was lost on the subject of his gaze.

"Why?" asked DeKok mildly.

The man in black made a vague gesture.

"I'm the doorman," he said.

"So, what?"

The man swallowed.

"You have to report to me, first."

DeKok shook his head.

"No way," he replied stubbornly. "First of all, a doorman is supposed to look like an admiral and stand at the door. It simply isn't done to sit in a glass booth in the middle of a reception hall. Secondly, our Commissaris said nothing about reporting to a doorman. We have an appointment with Mr. Bent."

"Oh."

"Yes, he's waiting for us."

The gentleman in black performed a measured bow.

"In that case I will announce the gentlemen. Who can I say?"

DeKok lifted his little felt hat in a polite gesture.

"My name is DeKok, with . . . eh, kay-oh-kay. This is my colleague, Vledder. We are, by the grace of our Chief Constable,* Detective-Inspectors attached to the Warmoes Street station."

The neatly dressed gentleman turned around and disappeared into the booth. Through the glass the two inspectors observed him making another bow while he spoke into the telephone. It was a comical sight. When the conversation had been concluded he emerged from his glass cage.

"Mr. Bent," he spoke self-importantly, "prefers to have his interview with the gentlemen elsewhere, not here in the office, but in his study at home. Mr. Bent will be down directly and lead the way."

Almost simultaneously with this announcement, they observed a muscular man descending by way of one of the marble staircases. He was a well-preserved man in his fifties with quick and athletic movements. He approached the two policemen with outstretched hand.

"I hope you won't mind coming home with me. I promised my wife I'd be home early." He made a joking gesture. "A promise to a beautiful woman has the force of Law."

DeKok looked at him.

"And what would you call the promise *from* a beautiful woman?"

The question seemed to touch Bent particularly. A hint of steel flickered momentarily in his eyes.

---

* Chief Constable: The highest rank in the Dutch police force. There is only one Chief Constable for all of Amsterdam. Other major cities and/or districts have their own Chief Constable. It is *not* a civilian rank.

"The promise *from* a beautiful woman," he answered thoughtfully and slowly, "is fleeting like perfume. It's seldom more than a sweet dream."

He seemed to be lost in thought. Then he laughed broadly.

"Would you gentlemen ride with me?"

DeKok nodded carelessly.

"As you wish," he drawled.

He never objected to meeting his potential opponents in their own surroundings. It sometimes gave him surprising insights.

* * *

Bent steered the big, heavy Bentley with a steady hand through the busy Amsterdam traffic. Meanwhile he talked lightly with Vledder next to him about various models of cars he had owned, or had tried out. He studiously avoided any reference to the hold-up. There was a painful silence when Vledder asked guilelessly what sort of car Bent thought most suitable for hold-ups.

The B&G president was visibly embarrassed by the question. But his confusion did not last long. He controlled himself almost immediately and remarked that he had never contemplated the use of any specific model in connection with a hold-up. DeKok did not participate in the conversation. He was comfortably ensconced on the back seat and listened. He was not particularly interested in the subject matter of the conversation, but he listened with considerable attention to the intonation of the words, the sound of the voices. In his opinion, Bent was less than straight-forward. The attitude of the president was too emphatically cheerful, too deliberately nonchalant. It was phony.

DeKok wondered what bothered the man. The hold-up? The loss of three million?

Bent's house was on the left side of the Amstel river, just outside the city limits. It was a splendid old villa with a thatched roof, partly hidden from view by a fine tangle of bare tree branches and twigs. Bent parked in a garage with an easy elan that showed much practice.

From the garage Bent led the way through an inside passage to a large room with big windows, that afforded a beautiful view of the river. To the left of the windows stood a solid, oak desk of immense proportions. It was heavily decorated with intricate carvings. The remaining walls of the room were covered from floor to ceiling with books and in the center of the room four easy chairs were grouped around a round table made of rare wood. A big, black tomcat was curled up in one of the chairs. It stood up, stretched itself and idly gazed at the visitors. For only a moment. Then the animal settled in its former position, yawned unashamedly and ignored the policemen. DeKok noticed the expression on the cat's face. It seemed to him as if the cat gave him a mocking grin.

Bent made an inviting gesture.

"Please sit down and excuse me for a moment. I'll be right back."

He left the room and DeKok stared after him. He admired the straight back, the athletic posture, the light thread and he concluded that Bent, despite his years, must have gone to considerable effort to keep fit. Rowing, perhaps, on the Amstel.

Bent returned to the study after a few minutes. He seemed dejected. There was a disappointed set to his mouth.

"I wanted to introduce you to my wife," he said morosely, "but she has gone to bed. She asks you to excuse her. She's not feeling well. A slight migraine, I think."

"I'm sorry to hear that," said DeKok with genuine sympathy. "We would have liked to meet her. Another time perhaps?"

Bent looked at him.

"Yes, yes," he answered absent-mindedly, "Another time." He dropped into one of the easy chairs. He looked suddenly very tired. He seemed a different person, older, more gray. "But to business," he said. His tone of voice had changed as well, had become more sharp, more incisive. "I take it that time is precious for you gentlemen?" The tone of voice did not match the expression on his face.

Vledder grinned.

"Yes," answered the young Inspector, "the lead the robbers have, increases with every minute's delay."

Bent nodded.

"I'm aware of that. Time is money. But I would appreciate it, if you could spare the time to listen to me."

He moved in his chair and brought his hands forward until the tips of his fingers rested against each other.

"Of course," he continued, "I don't know in what direction your investigations are leading, but I want to make it clear that our personnel, from high to low, is completely trustworthy. You might as well forget any possibility about a leak at B&G."

Vledder looked at the man with ill concealed surprise.

"And," he asked sarcastically, "is that all you have to tell us?"

A tic developed in one corner of Bent's mouth.

"Yes," he hesitated, "yes, that's about it, I think."

Vledder made an impatient gesture.

"And for this, ... this ... eh, *shocking* revelation you waste our valuable time and you drag us from the Emperor's Canal all the way to your house, here, on the Amstel?"

Bent nodded.

"Yes," he agreed emphatically, "for that remarkable revelation ..."

DeKok interrupted him smoothly.

"My young colleague means, of course, that your statement was superfluous. There was no need to tell us. The reliability and trustworthiness of your personnel was never an issue. B&G enjoys, also with the police, an outstanding reputation."

Bent looked suspiciously at DeKok and was apparently unsure how to react, at a loss for words.

"Thank you," he said finally.

At that moment, the black tomcat again rose, stretched its back high and lightly jumped down from the chair. It took the cat just a moment to make up its mind, then it jumped on Vledder's lap, turned a few times the way cats do and settled down in a comfortable position. Vledder softly scratched it under the chin. The animal started purring.

Bent looked at the cat and then at Vledder. The scene seemed to touch him and for just a moment he seemed to have forgotten all about the situation.

"It's strange," remarked the B&G president in a friendly tone of voice, "but whenever somebody sits down in *that* particular chair, he will always jump on that person's lap. I've noticed it many times. It's a peculiar habit. Not everybody likes cats."

DeKok coughed.

"In connection with the hold-up," he remarked in an apologetic tone, "we would like to ask you some questions, nevertheless." He smiled. "Just routine, you understand?"

Bent waved with a slender hand.

"Go ahead," he allowed.

"What," began DeKok, "determines the size of the shipments?"

"The need, the need of our offices, our clients."

DeKok nodded thoughtfully.

"Why did the truck stop behind the station, you don't have any clients there, do you?"

"No, this was a different kind of shipment, destined for Belgium. We have an arrangement with the railroads. Of course, one of our people usually accompanies the shipment."

"I see, but still a regular sort of shipment as far as you are concerned."

"Yes, the destination was different, that's all. I mean, it wasn't local."

"Yes?"

"We normally keep a large amount of cash in our vaults. Paper work and checks are generally distributed on an ongoing schedule, but cash can sometimes collect for a few days. In this case one of our clients requested us to prepare the shipment for Belgium."

"How did you come to have the money in the first place?

"It was collected from their branches in the normal way. We had simply not received instructions for delivery."

"Does that happen often?"

"Not often, but frequently enough to make it routine."

"And who knows what is needed, and where?"

Bent sighed.

"The managers of the various branches, of course, they prepare the requests."

DeKok smiled winningly.

"I understand. Every manager knows the requirements for his, or her, own office. But who knows the total?"

Bent shook his head.

"Only a few top people at the Emperor's Canal, at headquarters, know that exactly. The people who prepare the shipments, the drivers, they don't know. We like to remove temptation as much as possible."

"And for international shipments?"

"The same people and the instructing client, of course."

"So, it didn't mean a thing to the drivers that the amount was exceptionally high, this time?"

Bent made an annoyed gesture.

"Not in the least. They don't know the exact amount. As I said: they transport money. Just freight to them. That the amount was unusually high, this time . . . happens to be an unlucky coincidence."

DeKok laughed heartily.

"It depends, of course," he chuckled, "on one's point of view. The people who perpetrated the robbery, for instance, are probably pleasantly surprised." He paused, cocked his head and looked at the B&G president. Then he continued: "Unless, of course, unless it was *no* surprise to them at all, at all."

"What *do* you mean?"

DeKok shrugged his shoulders.

"Exactly what I'm saying. Perhaps they knew . . ."

Bent jumped up. His mouth formed a thin line across his face and there was an indignant fire in his eyes.

"You're insinuating . . ." He shouted. "You're insinuating that our company would . . . would be involved in . . . in . . ." His rage made him stutter and panting for breath, he stopped.

DeKok, too, stood up. Bent stood before him, red-faced with anger, his hands bunched into tight fists. DeKok suddenly realized how dangerous this man could be, especially in a fit of passion.

"Please, sit down," DeKok said soothingly. "There's no reason to get so excited. You read more in my words than I intended." He paused and gauged the effect of his words. Then he said: "By the way, Bent, I take it that the shipment was insured?"

It was a second attack on Bent's self-control. He lost that battle as well.

"Oh yes," he yelled, wildly gesticulating, "yes, the shipment was insured and the insurance company will pay." He leaned closer to DeKok, almost touching his face. "Is that another reason to suspect us? Our lawyers checked carefully. There's no financial damage to our company."

DeKok shook his head and sighed.

"I never worried about that for a moment," he said. He motioned toward Vledder. "Come on, Dick," he continued, "It's about time we were leaving. It would be impolite to impose any longer on the hospitality of Mr. Bent."

Vledder lifted the cat from his lap and handed the animal to the furious manager.

"In case you remember anything," said the young inspector politely, "that may help us in tracking down the perps, we'd be much obliged if you . . ."

Bent made a violent gesture.

"You may . . . you may . . ."

"May *what*, Mr. Bent?"

DeKok intervened. He was not interested in a permanent breach of communications. He always liked to leave an opening.

"I understand," he said pleasantly, "that the concerns of your company are close to your heart. We only want to find the perpetrators. That's the only purpose of our questions. There's absolutely no question of trying to blacken the name of your organization."

DeKok sighed. After everything that had been said, and thought, it was a lame speech. But the president became visibly calmer. The color drained from his face, his gestures became more controlled. He led Vledder and DeKok to the door.

The parting was cool, almost icy.

"I would appreciate," said Bent formally, "being kept informed of the progress of the case."

DeKok looked at him sharply.

"Even if, ... eh, if the developments take a turn that may be less pleasant for you?"

Bent pressed his lips together.

"Yes," he hissed, "then, too. Especially then."

The inspectors walked down the driveway. At the gate Vledder stopped to rub black cat hairs off his coat.

DeKok looked back at the house. His eyebrows rippled in amazement. He saw the slender shape of a young woman behind one of the windows of the study they had just left.

4

"Found out anything about the car, yet?"

Greanheather, the old desk-sergeant looked up absent-mindedly. With the pen still poised over the entry in the logbook, he stared at Vledder and DeKok.

"What car?" he asked finally.

"The car that was used in the hold-up, of course."

The desk-sergeant grinned.

"Oh," he said with a prim mouth, "you mean the Simca with NG-12-83. No, no news about that. The APB is still in force."

"What about the other Simca?"

Sergeant Greanheather pushed the logbook aside and pulled a folder in front of him. From that he produced a number of message flimsies.

"I read here," he said, "that only one of the two Simcas has been located so far. That's the blue Simca that was stolen from Heemstede, the suburb of Haarlem. The heavily damaged car was found on Route A-17 near Gouda. It had been driven head-on into one of the columns supporting an overpass. The front-end was caved in and the car is a total loss." He shook his head sadly, as if in commiseration. "Unfortunately, it wasn't the Simca you're after. The car still had its original license plates. Thus *not* NG-12-83. Also, there were no bullet holes in the trunk." He looked at the two inspectors. "And there should be, right?"

DeKok nodded.

"Indeed, there should be. Constable Bever is convinced that both his shots hit the trunk."

The sergeant pursed his lips.

"Well," he continued, "the lab guys had the crumpled Simca towed to headquarters, here in Amsterdam, and have gone over it with a fine tooth comb. They found no bullet holes of any kind." he paused. "Therefore," he continued pompously, "it has been established that the Simca that was stolen from Heemstede, was *not* the same vehicle that was used during the robbery. That leaves the Simca that was stolen from Haarlem."

"How terribly clever," remarked DeKok ironically.

Greanheather shrugged his wide shoulders nonchalantly.

"That," he observed evenly, "is to be expected from a good desk-sergeant."

Vledder laughed.

* * *

The large detective room on the third floor of the police station at Warmoes Street was empty when DeKok and Vledder entered. The other detectives had either gone home, or were on patrol somewhere within the inner city.

DeKok placed himself comfortably in his chair, put his feet on the desk and leisurely searched for a pack of gum. In his mind he went over the case. The near perfect execution, the unexpected large haul, the curious behavior of Mr. Bent. He had barely started and already a number of strange aspects had become evident. They were things that did not fit in the overall picture of the hold-up, things he did not like at all. Especially the fact that the car that was used for the robbery had not yet been found, caused his eyebrows to ripple in agitated nervousness.

It did not fit into the picture. It was unorthodox. Usually a stolen car was used for a robbery, or hold-up. That was hardly remarkable. It happened this time as well. But it was almost gospel that the suspects would get rid of the stolen car as soon as possible and then continue their flight in another, unregistered, unknown vehicle, a vehicle of which the license number was not known. That was the safest, the orthodox way of doing things. DeKok wondered why they had deviated from the safe way. Had something gone wrong? What was behind it? Of course, the license tags could have been changed, but then there remained the danger of driving around in a car with a description, a car with two bullet holes in the trunk. He rubbed his face with both hands and looked thoughtfully at Vledder, who had taken a seat across from him.

"The borders have been alerted?"

Vledder nodded emphatically.

"Oh, yes, the APB went out almost immediately and I specifically alerted the border posts. Of course, Interpol, too, was notified."

DeKok stared at nothing at all.

"Excellent," he answered vaguely, "really excellent." He scratched his neck pensively. "But I think we should have a little talk with the owner of the Simca in Haarlem."

Vledder looked at him with surprise.

"But why? What do you expect to gain by that? It's more than likely that the man has nothing to do with it. I mean, they needed a car for the hold-up. As it happens, somebody stole *his* car. That's all. It happens."

DeKok shook his head.

"It doesn't have to mean anything. I'm just surprised they haven't found his car yet. After all, Holland is so small, so densely populated and so well policed, they should have found *both* cars by now. Perhaps the owner can give us some additional details about the vehicle, some flaws, or something that makes the car stand out."

He rubbed his hands through his gray hair.

"Oh, yes," continued DeKok after a long pause, "there's something else I want. Try to get some background on Mrs. Bent."

"On who?"

DeKok smiled.

"Bent's wife. Wasn't that clear enough?"

Vledder grinned in surprise.

"Surely you don't think she has anything to do with it?"

"I don't know. Anything is possible. Behind every successful man, so they say, is a woman to inspire him. Sometimes it helps to know the source of the inspiration."

Vledder grimaced.

"The source is sick. You heard. She's in bed with migraine."

DeKok nodded slowly.

"That's what Bent wants us to believe. But when we left the villa this afternoon, there was a slender woman behind one of the windows of the study we had just left."

"Are you sure?"

"Absolutely."

"Perhaps a daughter?"

DeKok shook his head.

"I could be wrong, but she seemed too old to be a daughter. Besides, I don't think that Bent has any children living at home."

Vledder grinned.

"Well, back to *cherchez la femme*.* Who was the woman behind the window?"

* * *

The phone rang at that moment. DeKok lifted the receiver. Greanheather was on the other end.

"DeKok, you there?"

"Yes."

"There's a guy downstairs who wants to talk to you."

"Who is it?"

"Lowee. He says that's all the name you need."

DeKok laughed.

"That's right. Send him up."

Deep in thought, he replaced the receiver.

"Little Lowee is coming up."

Vledder nodded.

"I understand. I'll make myself scarce. Lowee *is* a bit shy and he's got only one friend with the police: the renowned sleuth, Detective-Inspector DeKok."

The younger man walked over to the coat rack and grabbed his coat.

"I'm going to Haarlem. I'll call you as soon as I know something."

DeKok waved goodbye.

---

* From the French: "look for the woman", an expression often used by the French police, because of the once popular belief that every (French) crime, somehow, was a crime of passion.

45

* * *

DeKok feigned pure amazement when Little Lowee, a bit reluctantly, entered the detective room.

"What's the matter, Lowee?" he asked. "If I feel like a cognac, you don't have to deliver. I'll be happy to come and get it."

Little Lowee sank down on a chair next to DeKok's desk and worried nervously with his fingers of which the nails had been bitten to the quick.

"Please, no jokes, Mr. DeKok," he said anxiously. "I don't have a lotta time. I can't stay away too long. You see, somebody is watching the bar and you never know, they steal you blind before you know it."

DeKok moved his eyebrows in that inimitable manner.

"So, why are you here?"

Lowee's adam's apple bobbed up and down.

"I've been worrying about it all afternoon. It nags, you know what I mean? I'm just *that* worried about it, Mr. DeKok."

"About what?"

Lowee rubbed the back of his hand along his dry lips.

"Lookit, Mr. DeKok, you asked me this morning iffen I had seen anything of Cunning Pete, lately."

"Yes?"

"Well, eh, I said no, because I thought you were lookin' for 'im, you know."

"So, what?"

Little Lowee pulled a sad face.

"I lied, you understand. But it was a good lie, I mean, I thought I was doing the right thing. I seen him a lot, you see. He usta come a lot, lately."

"Go on."

46

"Yes." The small barkeeper remained silent and stared into the distance. "You see," he continued, "I wouldn't have told you, normally . . . but Pete is dead now." He lowered his narrow chin toward his chest and rubbed his eyes. There was no doubt that the tiny barkeeper was genuinely moved. "Pete," he continued finally, with a sob in his voice, "Pete usta tell stories, you know." He made a helpless gesture. "Mostly people just *asked* to be lied to, you know. But in his heart, deep down, Pete was a honest guy. Really." He blinked his eyes, as if to remove a tear. "I swear to you, Mr. DeKok, Pete was as honest as the day is long."

DeKok looked mockingly at the barkeeper.

"What do you want from me, Lowee? Should I cry, now?"

Lowee sprang up and banged his fist on the desk with surprising strength.

"It's a damn rotten trick they pulled on that boy, you know that?" His voice was loud and his face was distorted by fury. "Yessir, a damn rotten trick," he repeated.

DeKok bit his lower lip.

"Yes, to stick somebody from behind with a dagger, yes, Lowee, I agree, that's a damn rotten trick."

Little Lowee nodded sadly.

"And all for a coupla bucks."

DeKok did not react immediately.

"A . . . eh, a few bucks?" he asked finally.

Lowee ground his teeth.

"Yes, no more than a few filthy bucks. They wanted to cut him out, I bet. Didn't want to share the loot."

"Share?"

"Yep, they wanted to cut him out. It's obvi . . . , eh, obvi . . . eh, it's as clear as anything. You see, Pete knew all about the hold-up."

DeKok kept his face expressionless. He succeeded with considerable difficulty.

"You're telling me," he said slowly, "that Pete knew about the hold-up?"

Lowee nodded vehemently.

"He tole me hisself."

"How did he know?"

"From the guys." Lowee made an impatient gesture.

"What guys?"

"Geez, DeKok, the guys that were to do the job, of course."

"And they are?"

"Iffen I knew that, DeKok ... iffen I knew that ... I woulda told you. Really. If only outa revenge for Pete." He looked at the inspector, his head cocked to one side. "You believes me, don't you?"

DeKok nodded slowly.

"Yes, Lowee, I believe that," he replied formally.

For a long time they sat silently opposite each other. Each occupied by his own thoughts. Above their heads the defective ballast in one of the light fixtures hummed annoyingly. A drunk in the street tried to sing a melancholy song about dying and crying and trains.

Slowly Lowee rose from his chair.

"I can't stay any longer," he said somberly. "I gotta get back."

DeKok nodded pensively.

"Before you go, Lowee, one more question. Was Pete planning to participate in the hold-up?"

Lowee shook his head.

"Nah, you shoulda known that yourself, DeKok. A hold-up, with guns and all. That wasn't Pete's style. Pete was a story teller, all right, a con-man, but never any violence. He

48

never liked violence. He just *talked* people outa their money."

* * *

With a tired gesture, DeKok rubbed his face with both hands.

"Did Pete tell you how large the haul was going to be?"

A thoughtful expression appeared on the friendly, mousy face of Little Lowee.

"Yeah, wait a minute, he talked about that. At least half a million, he said. Nowheres near three million as it says in the papers." He suddenly looked searchingly at DeKok. "Say, that three million ain't no funny stuff of you guys, is it?"

"What do you mean?"

"Now, to make the guys go crazy, of course."

"How so?"

"Geez, DeKok, you're real dense today. I mean, half a million is gone, you guys make it three million. Before you knows it, the guys are fighting with each other about the missing loot. One may get pissed enough to tell you about it."

DeKok shook his head.

"No, there really seems to be three million on the loose."

Lowee whistled between his teeth.

"Nice day's work."

DeKok laughed.

"So, Cunning Pete really believed the haul wouldn't be much bigger that five hundred thousand?"

"Yes."

"But Pete did want to share in part of it?"

"I think so, yes."

"Why?"

Lowee shrugged his shoulders.

"Because he knew about it, of course."

"That's the only reason?"

"Yes."

"Hush money," grinned DeKok.

"You mean, he was gonna talk, otherwise?"

"Exactly."

Lowee shook his head.

"Never. Pete wouldn't do such a thing."

"He could have threatened it."

Lowee made an annoyed gesture.

"Pete wasn't that sort. Nossir. He wasn't a canary. I tole you: Pete was as honest as the day is long. He just figured on some pocket money, that's all."

DeKok sighed.

"But why did Pete tell you about it?"

Again Lowee shrugged his narrow shoulders.

"Ach, you know how it goes. A drink, pissed off, another drink . . . and then come the tales . . ."

DeKok nodded his understanding. He stood up and placed a fatherly hand on the slight shoulders of the small barkeeper.

"Thanks for coming," he said simply.

Lowee walked toward the door with bent head. Halfway to the door he stopped, turned around and walked back to the desk. He stopped in front of the gray sleuth.

"I . . . eh, I don't always agree with you, DeKok." His voice quivered with emotion. "Most of the time I don't, I should say. But this time, yes, this time, I hope you get them bastards real quick."

DeKok gave him a friendly grin.

"I'll do my best, Lowee."

After the barkeeper had left, DeKok sat down again. He held his head between his hands, the elbows on the edge of the desk.

He let the entire conversation with Lowee pass in review. Every word, every intonation, every gesture was remembered. Not in his wildest imagination would he have suspected that there was a connection between the murder of Pete Geffel and the hold-up. It had been a complete revelation. There remained the question about the exact relationship between the two events. What *had* been Pete's role? Of course, Pete was usually involved in some sort of semi-respectable business. It *was* his business. He was a con-man, one of the best. *Honest as the day was long.* Lowee's testimonial could hardly be taken seriously. It was no more, nor less, than an obituary for a dead partner in crime. After all, thought DeKok, in addition to his apparently respectable front as a barkeeper, Lowee had, at one time or another, broken nearly all of God's Commandments. It was certain that he still dealt in stolen goods; was, in fact, one of the foremost fences of the Quarter. Pete, also, was more than an ordinary con-man. His actions sometimes hovered dangerously close to blackmail. It was not at all unlikely that someone had seen Pete's death as the only possible solution to his, or her, own problems. Blackmailers led a precarious life.

But, when all was said and done, the fact that Pete Geffel knew about the plans for the hold-up was enough reason for DeKok to get involved with the murder in Seadike. Despite the warning from the Commissaris to the contrary. And that, in itself . . .

His thoughts were interrupted by the ringing of the telephone. He lifted the receiver. An excited Vledder was on the other end of the line.

"Guess what?"

"You call me to play guessing games?"

"The Simca 1500 that was stolen from Haarlem, belongs to a certain Bergen."

"So?"

"You know who Bergen is?"

"Not yet."

"One of the managers of B&G."

"What!?"

"Yes, one of the people who knew that this particular transport was heavy on cash. He knew about the three million."

5

DeKok gave Vledder a hearty welcome.

"I'm glad you got back so quickly, from Haarlem," he called jovially. "You see, I want to pay another visit to Mother Geffel."

Vledder unbuttoned his coat.

"Mother Geffel?"

"Yes."

"Tonight still?"

"Yes."

"A condolence visit?"

DeKok nodded slowly.

"You could call it that, yes, to express our sympathy."

Vledder looked at him suspiciously. His sharp eyes took in DeKok's innocent face. He tried to read the true meaning behind the bald statement. But DeKok's friendly face did not reveal any answers.

"I should remind you," grinned Vledder, "that the Commissaris has prohibited you from any participation in the Geffel case."

DeKok pushed his lower lip forward and shook his head.

"I . . . eh, I don't think I can obey the Commissaris in this."

Vledder looked at him in astonishment.

"Why not?"

"Because Pete Geffel knew everything about the hold-up."

"What!?"

"Yes, in a confidential mood, he told Little Lowee all about it."

For a moment Vledder was speechless. In a series of quick, brief thought associations he tried to incorporate the news into the overall picture he had built up so far.

"Is that why Pete was killed?"

"What, why?"

"Because he knew about the hold-up."

"I don't think so," answered DeKok pensively. "I don't think it was that. The mere fact that he knew about the hold-up would not have been enough reason to kill him. There must have been more who knew about the hold-up, friends, family of the crooks and so on. As a rule they don't keep their mouth shut, they like to boast."

"Perhaps Pete threatened to betray them."

DeKok cocked his head at his younger colleague. His eyebrows rippled briefly.

"Even *before* the hold-up?"

"Yes."

DeKok shook his head.

"No, Dick. Pete would never have been *that* dumb. It wasn't for nothing that he was known as *Cunning* Pete. He had quite a reputation in the underworld." He raised a finger in the air. "I'm almost positive that if Pete had the idea to make some money from his knowledge, he would have waited until *after* the hold-up. He would have had all the time in the world to make his demands and, a secure feeling for a blackmailer, would have known that his victims had the means to pay him. Considering the haul they made, they might not even have minded, not much, anyway." He paused and drummed his fingers on the desk. "Still," he continued after a while, "Pete was killed on the night *before* the hold-up. And that's rather strange."

Vledder shrugged his shoulders.

"Perhaps the guys who did the hold-up anticipated Pete's blackmail attempt and just got him out of the way to be on the safe side. You know, just as a precaution."

DeKok bit his lower lip.

"Possibly," he said, deep in thought, "just maybe. But it does seem rather far-fetched. I mean, kill somebody before he has even done anything? That's ... eh, that's just *too* precipitous. There has to be another, more reasonable motive."

"All right, what?"

DeKok ambled over to the coat rack.

"If you've got trouble sleeping, tonight, meditate upon that question."

He pulled on his coat, pressed his little, old felt hat on top of his head.

"Come on, we'll go see Mother Geffel."

Vledder followed without protest.

* * *

Ever since her wedding day, old lady Geffel had lived in the small, spotless house on the quiet side of the Lily Canal. The house always smelled of coffee and furniture polish. A rather heavy-set neighbor woman opened the door. She raised her eyebrows with a questioning expression when she saw the two inspectors on the doorstep. DeKok lifted his hat.

"We . . . eh," he said hesitatingly, "we want to express our sympathy to Mrs. Geffel about the loss of her son."

The neighbor pressed her heavy body against the side of the corridor.

"Please come in," she said, "she's inside."

There were a lot of people in the small living room. Family, friends and acquaintances with sad faces. Mother Geffel was seated in a chair next to the window. When DeKok entered she looked at him with a teary face. For just a moment it seemed as if she would cry again. But she controlled herself and with surprising strength she gripped both hands of the gray sleuth.

"I always warned my Pete, Mr. DeKok," she said sadly. "You know that. I always said he would come to a bad end. But he would never listen, not to me, or to anybody. He always knew everything better."

She shook her head.

"And how much did Uncle Gus Shenk not do for him? Ever since my husband died, he always kept an eye on the boy. But all for nothing. He always thought that life was nothing but a game and all the people in the world were there only to amuse Pete Geffel."

Her voice sounded bitter.

"Oh, yes," she went on in a changed tone, "they always did laugh at his jokes, his tricks. They laughed too much you know. That was the problem. It was that way when he was only a kid and he was always the center of attention. We never saw how wrong that could be. First it was Funny Pete, then Handy Pete and finally just Cunning Pete. You see, that's how it happened. It became worse all the time and it's my fault. From the beginning I should have been much more strict ..."

DeKok placed one of his large hands tenderly on the shoulder of the old woman.

"I wouldn't blame myself too much if I were you, Mrs. Geffel. There's no reason for that at all, at all. It's *not* your fault and I know that." He sighed. "How could you have prevented his death? How? You could hardly keep him by the hand all the time. There was no way to tie him to your apron strings. No, Pete was old enough and wise enough to take care of himself."

The old woman sobbed softly.

"And lately there was such an improvement. I was so happy. After all, you *do* want what's best for your child, don't you? He had met a girl, a nice, kind girl. He would do anything for her. I'd never seen anything like it. He couldn't care less about girls, as a rule. But this one was different. He even contacted an employment agency, looking for regular work."

DeKok's eyebrows danced briefly across his forehead.

"Work?" he asked.

"Oh, yes, he had serious plans."

"Marriage?"

"Yes."

"What's the name of the girl?"

"Florentine ... Florentine La Croix."

"A beautiful name," admired DeKok.

A vague smile fled across the wrinkled face of the old woman.

"But he didn't call her Florentine. That was too ostentatious, he said. He called her Flossie ... just Flossie." She gestured. "That was my Pete. That was his way. He had a special name for everybody and everything." She looked up at him, a bit shyly, a hint of a naughty twinkle in her eye. "He had a special name for you too," she said. "He called you *the Cocque of the walk*. He was so clever. He frenchified your name, you see," she explained superfluously. "Cocque means *rooster* in French, you see, and thus . . ."

"Yes, yes," said DeKok hastily, casting a warning glance at a smirking Vledder. He was well aware of Vledder's opinion regarding the similarity in names between himself and the very late Captain Banning Cocq. "Did . . . eh," he continued, "did he talk about me at all, lately?"

She looked at him, wondering about the question.

"You mean," she said finally, slowly, "about you being after him?" Then, in response to DeKok's nod, she continued: "No, as I said, things were going so much better."

DeKok nodded again.

"Do you know who he hung around with, lately?"

"No, I don't. Anyway, I never knew that. Those sort of things he kept from me, you see. He knew what I thought about his so-called friends."

DeKok remained silent. His glance roamed the small room, observed those present. He saw a few old acquaintances. There was Old Bill, who he had arrested once, a long time ago, for dealing in stolen goods. And "Uncle" Derek. Uncle Derek Geffel who, despite his sixty years, still liked to get involved in street fights. Just some old, semi-retired ex-cons who were past it. There were no modern criminals present.

DeKok shook hands with the old lady.

"When is the funeral?"

Mother Geffel swallowed.

"Thursday, . . . this Thursday at Sorrow Field."

DeKok rubbed his dry lips with the back of his hand.

"I'll try to be there and I'll see if Uncle Gus Shenk wants to come as well. You know how he liked the boy."

Mother Geffel searched for a handkerchief.

A murmur of agreement went through the room.

* * *

DeKok guided the police VW along the Amsterdam canals. He was not in a hurry. His head burst with ideas. Once in while he would look at young Vledder, slouched in the seat beside him.

"What's the matter. Dick?" he asked at last. "Something bothering you?"

Vledder pressed himself more or less into a sitting position.

"It just doesn't compute," he said, irritation in his voice. "If Mother Geffel is right and if Pete was in the process of changing his lifestyle, well, then his death becomes an even greater puzzle than it is already. For one thing, what's left of a motive?"

DeKok searched for, and found, a stick of chewing gum.

"You never know," he said somberly. "Perhaps his 'conversion' is the motive for the killing." He sighed deeply, clamping down on the chewing gum. "Anyway," he continued, "keep in mind that a mother usually presents her son in as good a light as possible. I wouldn't take all her statements as Gospel, you know. His reform is nothing knew ... it's happened before. Ask Shenk, he'll tell you."

For a time they drove along in silence. Between them hung the spirit of Cunning Pete. DeKok was the first to break the silence.

"Apart from your brief phone call," he began, "I haven't heard anything about your visit to Haarlem."

"Ach," answered Vledder, irked. "There's not all that much to tell. First I went to the local police station and they provided me with an escort to point out the house. It was a nice house, a big house, in the suburbs."

"With a garage?"

"No, no, it was an old-fashioned house. No garage. That's why the Simca was parked in the street."

"What was your impression of Bergen?"

"Oh, a nice guy. He told me of his own accord that he was one of the managers at B&G. He certainly didn't make a secret of it. But ... he said: 'you must not give that any particular significance. The fact that a blue Simca was used during the hold-up and the fact that I happen to own a blue Simca that has been stolen, is no more than a peculiar coincidence of circumstances and you, detectives, must not assume that it is anything more than that'."

DeKok laughed.

"Did you learn that by heart?"

Vledder smiled.

"Believe me, that's exactly the way he said it. I thought is so beautifully phrased that I remembered it."

"And what did Mrs. Bergen say?"

Vledder turned abruptly toward DeKok

"My goodness, good thing you reminded me, I'd almost forgotten. Mrs. Bergen made a particularly strange remark."

"Remark?"

"Yes, she said, and I quote: 'Bent should never have married for the second time.'."

"What did that have to do with anything?"

Vledder gestured.

"It had absolutely nothing to do with anything. That's the point. It was just an idle remark, without reason, or purpose. Bergen, quite rightly I think, ignored it. He just gave her an angry look. Obviously he wasn't happy with the remark."

"What next?"

"Nothing next. I tried to get the conversation on the subject of Bent, I tried several times. But without success. Bergen didn't give me a chance. After his wife's remark he firmly kept the trend of the conversation under control. It was almost as if he was afraid she would say anything else. Of course, I could have directed a number of pertinent questions at her, but I didn't want to be obvious."

DeKok nodded his understanding.

"Time enough for that."

He parked the car along the sidewalk.

"You're home," he said. "Get a good night's sleep and then, in the morning, off you go to Seadike. I want you to personally acquaint yourself with the facts. Especially the technical details are important to me, you know, footprints, fingerprints, special characteristics of the weapon . . . There must be a lot of detail that simply wasn't included in the telex message this morning."

Vledder smiled. DeKok would insist on calling a fax a telex. He got out of the car.

"What's your next step?" he asked from the sidewalk.

DeKok shook his head.

"I think I'll just stop by the office for a moment, on my way home, just to double check on new developments, if any."

Vledder nodded.

"And what about Mrs. Bergen's remark?"

DeKok smiled.

61

"We take it at face value. Perhaps Bent *shouldn't* have married for the second time."

* * *

DeKok proceeded at a snail's pace in fourth gear. The old engine in the VW protested vehemently. DeKok ignored it. Engines were not a passion with him and he felt even less sympathy for transmissions. Quietly he bounced along.

When he spotted a phone booth at the corner of the Roses Canal and the Wester Market, he suppressed with difficulty the malicious impulse to call the Commissaris out of bed. He would have liked to tell him that he was, after all, going to get involved with Pete Geffel's murder. He grinned softly at himself, then reflected that it would be bad manners to disturb the well deserved rest of the old man and passed the phone booth with a soft glow of inner righteousness.

He parked the car behind the building and walked toward the front of the station house. Suddenly he heard the unmistakable tick-tack of high heels behind him. He looked over his shoulder and saw a beautiful blonde girl, dressed in a long, black cape.

"DeKok?"

He nodded, hesitatingly.

"With ... eh, with kay-oh-kay," he answered, almost mechanically. Another beautiful blonde, he thought. And then, with an inner shrug, he thought, what else can you expect in Holland? Curiously he looked at the young woman.

She gave him a sweet smile.

"I'm Flossie."

6

DeKok leaned his elbows on the desk. From over his folded hands he looked with approval at the young woman across the desk from him. His first impression had been correct, he determined. She *was* beautiful, extraordinarily beautiful. She had sparkling blue eyes, a clear, open face and an ivory skin. Her long, blonde hair came down in luxurious waves and contrasted pleasantly with the black cape.

At first he had estimated her to be younger, but now, in the detective room, under the harsh lights of the neon tubes she looked to be about twenty-four, maybe twenty-five years old. He tried to remember if he had ever met her before, but again he thought, not without irony, that fate had led a lot of beautiful blonde women to cross his path. It was almost an occupational hazard, he reflected ruefully. His experiences were mixed. Beautiful women showed a sometimes frightening willingness to get involved in all sorts of difficulties. But that was definitely the only objection DeKok had against beautiful women.

"I waited a long time for you."

She had a deep, sultry voice that echoed softly and pleasantly in the room.

"I'm sorry," sighed DeKok. "After all, I wasn't to know that . . ."

She waved his apologies away.

"I take it you know who I am?"

DeKok swallowed.

"Flossie . . . isn't that what you said?"

With a nonchalant gesture she shrugged off her cape, shook her long hair and adjusted the hem of her skirt. Her long, slender legs were stunning.

"Florentine La Croix. Flossie . . . Flossie is just for my most intimate friends." She smiled at him sweetly and pulled her chair a little closer. "So to you . . . I'm Flossie."

DeKok took refuge in his puritanical, civil servant soul and braced himself for what was to come next. He decided, no matter what, not to succumb to the undeniable attraction of the young woman.

"Flossie."

His voice sounded strange to him. To hide his inner confusion he rummaged in a drawer, then sat back.

"I am . . . I *was* a friend of Pete Geffel."

DeKok nodded slowly, regaining his self-control.

"I know," he answered. "Mother Geffel told me." He hesitated a moment. "I had imagined you different," he added.

She smiled charmingly.

"A different image?"

DeKok pushed his lower lip forward.

"Yes, Mother Geffel spoke of a kind girl, a nice girl to whom Pete was devoted."

She gave him a challenging look.

"Something wrong with that?"

DeKok made an apologetic gesture.

"No, no, nothing. It's my fault. Apparently I have a limited imagination."

She looked at him searchingly. The expression on her face became more formal. The smile had disappeared.

"What do you mean?"

DeKok shrugged his shoulders reluctantly.

"Well, you don't exactly look the picture of what I had imagined: a kind, nice girl, a girl who mourns the passing of her friend."

She twiddled nervously with a button of her blouse. A red blush spread over her cheeks.

"What do you expect me to do?" she asked vehemently "Perhaps you expect me to sit here sucking my thumb, or to cry on your shoulder. Is that what you want?"

"Why not? I don't mind. Go ahead." He nodded encouragingly at her, his eyes half closed. "It's a relief, believe me. And don't worry about your make-up. Go ahead and cry, if you want to. You don't have to be attractive or alluring for me. I'm just a civil servant so it's all wasted on me, anyway."

She moved in her chair.

"You won't see me cry," she said, a determined tone in her voice.

DeKok shrugged his shoulders.

"As you like," he remarked resignedly. "Nobody's forcing you."

She did not react.

DeKok looked at her with interest. Even with a determined, stubborn look on her face, she was gorgeous, impressive.

"You called him 'Peter', is that right?"

"Yes."

"Did you love him?"

"Yes."

"You knew about his past?"

She nodded.

"Everything, from the moment he was born," she admitted.

"Well, and?"

She looked at him, frowning angrily. Her eyes spat fire.

"What do you mean: well, and?" Her tone was rebellious. "What's that supposed to mean, eh? I loved Peter. I told you, didn't I?"

DeKok avoided her penetrating look, the angry eyes. He understood at once that he had found a weak spot in her armor. Always the policeman, he wondered how to use it, how long it would be before she gave up all resistance.

"So, Pete's past did not affect your relationship with him?"

She hesitated for a moment.

"It didn't hurt us," she said softly.

DeKok slapped his flat hand on the top of the desk. The sound made her jump. His face was angry.

"That's not what I asked," he said, louder than intended. "I didn't ask whether it did, or did not hurt you, I asked if it affected you."

Her lips trembled.

"Yes, it affected us."

Her attitude changed visibly, it became softer, less rigid. For the first time DeKok detected something of the "kind, nice girl" described by Mother Geffel. He regretted his loss of control, the momentary outburst.

"You tried," he said in a friendly tone of voice, "to change Pete's attitude, to change his lifestyle?"

She nodded slowly.

"Yes," she answered softly, "I tried to do that."

"And you counted on his feelings for you?"

"Yes."

DeKok sighed.

"And yet, the hold-up happened," he said.

Suddenly she lost all self-control, all resistance seemed to dissipate. Her body shook noticeably and tears filled her eyes. They dribbled down her cheeks and fell on the folded hands in her lap.

"Yes, it happened," she sobbed. "It happened." Wildly she shook her head. "That ... that was the worst of all. Believe me, that was the worst of all."

DeKok's eyebrows rippled briefly. There was nobody to be amazed at the sight.

"Worse than Pete's death?"

The question struck her like a blow to the body. She clapped both hands to her face and started to cry in earnest. She wailed out her sorrow with long moans and shrieks. She was hyper-ventilating and seemed inconsolable.

DeKok let her be. The outburst had not surprised him. After a while he stood up, went to the water fountain and poured her a glass of water. Her teeth rattled against the glass while she drank.

"He promised me he promised me he promised me," she repeated over and over.

DeKok looked at her intently for some time, his head cocked to one side.

"What ... eh, what did he promise you?"

"That he would call."

"Call who?"

"The Company."

DeKok had difficulty swallowing.

"B&G?"

She looked at him with a teary face.

67

"Yes, the money transport."

The gray sleuth rubbed his hands over his burning eyes. Suddenly he felt tired, exhausted. From between his fingers he looked at the young woman. It hurt him to see her in such a state. Slowly he pulled a clean handkerchief from his pocket and handed it to her.

"Come on, Flossie," he said encouragingly, "wipe your tears. You were so resolute when you first came in."

A hint of a smile broke through her features. It was as if she suddenly remembered her entrance into the room.

"Yes, I planned for you and me . . . and if you didn't want that . . . to go after him alone, after the murderer of my Peter."

DeKok looked at her with astonishment.

"Is that why you came?"

She cleaned her face.

"Yes, that's why I came. I wanted to work with you, help you." She picked nervously at the wrinkled handkerchief in her hand. "And I am *still* determined to find Peter's murderer."

DeKok ignored the remark with his usual, supreme indifference. As if she had said nothing else, he continued:

"So, Peter had promised you to phone B&G." His tone was matter-of-fact, businesslike.

"Yes."

"Why?"

She made a vague gesture.

"To warn them . . . to warn them that a hold-up, a robbery, had been planned. We discussed it for hours, he and I."

"When was that?"

"Last week. Peter knew that some guys had a plan to hold up the transport of that company. He told me. He had no secrets from me, he always told me everything. He also told me how he could make some money from the hold-up."

"Blackmail?"

She nodded timidly.

"That's what it's called, I think. You see, after the hold-up had succeeded he wanted those guys to share with him. Not a lot, just enough to buy a few things and to get married."

"And?"

She made a violent gesture.

"I didn't want to hear about it."

"Didn't you want to get married?"

"Of course I did. I would have liked nothing better than to get married. But not with money from crime. You can see that, can't you, that's no way to start a marriage." There was genuine indignation in her voice. "I told Peter," she continued, "that if he was really serious about me, if he wanted to change his life, then *here* was the chance to prove it. To make me believe him."

DeKok nodded, staring out of the window.

"You meant, I take it, that warning B&G could be the first good deed on his part, the first step, so to speak, on the path to a better, a more law-abiding life? To put an end to the past, to start anew."

"Exactly."

DeKok pulled thoughtfully on his lower lip.

"But why not inform the police? That would be the logical thing to do . . . ."

She shook her head, interrupting him.

"That's what I suggested, but Peter wouldn't hear of it."

"Why not?"

She looked at DeKok, a bit shy, embarrassed.

"Peter said that he was too familiar with police methods. They would, he explained, calmly stand by while the hold-up progressed just so they could catch the guys in the act. He didn't want that."

"And then Pete promised you that he would call the company, phone B&G?"

For just a moment it seemed as if she would start to cry again, but she regained her composure.

"That's what he promised," she whispered.

DeKok nodded.

"And then," he continued gravely, "when you heard that an armed robbery had been committed that afternoon, you felt betrayed. Betrayed by your own Peter Geffel." He sighed deeply. "And that hurt more than the fact that somebody stabbed him to death with a dagger."

She lowered her head, the blonde hair fell like a curtain in front of her face. She nodded almost imperceptibly.

"*That* hurt, yes."

DeKok rose with some difficulty from his chair and began to pace up and down the large detective room.

"But the question remains," he observed after a while, "if your conclusion is correct."

She turned to face him abruptly.

"What do you mean?"

DeKok made a vague gesture.

"The question remains if you drew the right conclusion," he repeated. "The fact that the hold-up took place, nevertheless, does *not* necessarily mean that Pete didn't keep his promise to you."

"I don't understand," she said slowly. "If Peter had called, the company would have taken measures, surely? I mean, . . . the robbers would never have been able to take off with three million . . ."

70

DeKok smiled.

"Let's not discuss it any further," he said in a friendly tone of voice. "It's quite late, you know." He pointed at the large clock on the wall. "It's way past two in the morning. I'll take you home. You've had a terrible day. It's about time you get a good night's rest."

Her face fell.

"I don't want to go home," she said moodily. "I can't sleep, anyway."

DeKok ambled over to the coat rack and pulled on his coat. Then he picked up the heavy cape and placed it over her shoulders.

"I'll take you to Mother Geffel," he said soothingly. "That's perhaps better. Try to console the old lady a bit, if you can."

She shook her head.

"No, not to Mother Geffel. Take me home, after all. I still have to take care of Doug."

"Doug?"

A wan smile brightened her beautiful face briefly.

"My cat."

She rose slowly.

"How can I help you find Peter's murderer?"

DeKok gave her a long, penetrating look.

"Give me the names of the men who were going to do the hold-up."

He read fear in her eyes.

"I don't know them. Really, Mr. DeKok, I don't know who they are. Peter never mentioned their names."

7

It was closer to eleven than to half past ten the next morning when DeKok, his decrepit little felt hat nonchalantly on the back of his head, entered the police station at Warmoes Street in a jovial mood.

When he took his shower earlier, he had entertained himself with loud singing, then he had consumed a leisurely and extensive breakfast, after which he and his faithful dog, a sad-looking boxer with a worried face, had gone for a long walk. The dog looked as if it was doing most of the thinking for DeKok, but was mainly interested in the trees in the park and the black poodle from next door.

In many ways DeKok looked like his dog, or the other way around. The similarity between DeKok and his dog was striking: they shared solemn looking faces and playful personalities. DeKok did not share the dog's interest in trees. The intelligent animal was aware of that. It was a constant source of sorrow to the dog, but, as is the way of dogs, this flaw in DeKok's character was no reason for the dog to be any less devoted and faithful to its master.

DeKok had been thinking about the case on the way to the office. That is, when he finally made his way to the office. The fact that the robbers must so far have used every available minute to hide their loot, could not spoil his good humor. That was all right with him. As far as DeKok was concerned, money was not something to get all worked up about. Crimes involving just money, had never been able to get his full interest. He simply could not get too excited over the 'Mine and Thine' of things. If Pete Geffel's death had not been involved with the robbery, one way or the other, he would have just handled the case routinely, closed it routinely and moved on to other things. But it was different now. The murder had complicated the case, had added spice to the problems surrounding it. It drove him to solve the puzzles that had been created. And there were so many puzzles. For instance, if he reflected on the calm, professional, non-violent way in which the robbery had taken place, it was difficult to reconcile that with a dagger in the back of Cunning Pete. And that was but *one* of the puzzles that occupied him.

He quickly suppressed a fleeting thought that both cases, after all, had nothing to do with each other. There had to be a connection. There simply *had* to be. That conviction was impossible to eradicate from his mind. Nevertheless, the question remained: how were they connected?

Inspector Corstant laughed at DeKok when he entered the detective room and gave him a cheery wave.

"The Commissaris has been asking for you. You had to report at once." Corstant paused and grinned broadly. "That was more than an hour ago," he added.

DeKok aimed his little hat at the peg where he normally hung it. As usual, he missed. He bent over and retrieved the article. Not in the least put out, he hung it on the peg. Only then did he respond to Corstant's announcement.

"Oh, well, in that case it's old news," he said, divesting himself of his coat.

74

Corstant grinned again.

"But I wouldn't keep him waiting," he responded earnestly. "I have the feeling that the old man is rather pissed. When I told him you weren't here, he asked for Vledder. When I explained, respectfully, that he wasn't here either, I could not shake the impression that he might, mind you, *might* have used a . . . eh, a strong word."

DeKok shook his head sadly.

"The Commissaris must be associating with bad companions."

* * *

DeKok knocked discreetly on the door and entered. He was at a loss to understand what the Commissaris could possibly want from him. There was no way that the old man had gotten wind of the latest developments. It had to be something else.

The tall, stately police chief was seated behind his desk like an angry father confronting a wayward child. He seemed absorbed in a file. When he finally looked up, his face had assumed a pensive expression.

"I called you because . . ."

DeKok kept his gaze aimed about two inches above the head of the Commissaris. He was familiar with that opening. It was the beginning of a reprimand, at the very least, an expression of the old man's displeasure. Suddenly he discovered an excellent reproduction of a Monet above and behind the head of the Commissaris. He had never noticed that before.

"Excellent," remarked DeKok, "really excellent. I didn't know you were interested in art."

The Commissaris, distracted from his train of thought by the interruption, made an angry gesture.

"Yes, well, the building people hung it there." His voice was irritated. "It wouldn't have been my choice."

DeKok's eyebrows rippled briefly, almost unnoticeably. The Commissaris could not suppress a quick, startled look.

"You don't appreciate it?" asked DeKok.

The Commissaris moved in his chair.

"Monet was," said the Commissaris, "to the best of my knowledge, an impressionist. I don't like impressionists." He aimed his penetrating look at DeKok and continued: "Look at the painting," he pontificated, "impressions are always vague, unclear. They form a nebulous territory, a territory in which an inspector can easily get lost."

"I have the feeling," grinned DeKok, "that you are trying to tell me something."

The Commissaris nodded.

"That feeling is correct, DeKok. I just want to convey to you that, if it's your impression that those responsible for the B&G hold-up, should be found within the company, rather than outside of the company, you are indulging in a strictly personal impression. That's all."

DeKok lowered his head.

"That's all," he repeated calmly. Then: "I have a strong suspicion that you've been approached by Mr. Bent."

The Commissaris coughed discreetly.

"Indeed," he said reluctantly. "Mr. Bent called me last night. He is seriously upset about your behavior, the behavior of both of you, you *and* Vledder. Especially the sarcastic tone of young Vledder offended him deeply. It struck him as extremely unpleasant."

DeKok grinned broadly. His grin was irresistible. It transformed his somewhat melancholy face into one of boyish delight. It was one of his most attractive features. But the Commissaris remained unaffected.

"Well . . . well," said DeKok in a mocking tone of voice, "Mr. Bent has been deeply offended. He was struck unpleasantly. How would he have preferred to be struck?"

The commissarial face assumed a disapproving look.

"You know very well what I mean." His tone was sharp.

DeKok shrugged his shoulders.

"Mr. Bent has no grounds for complaints," he answered calmly. "Vledder's remarks were completely justified."

The Commissaris made a negating gesture.

"Justified, or . . . not justified," his voice took on the affected speech of the consummate civil servant, became sententious. "Civil servants, servants of the public," he continued, "must, under all circumstances behave themselves according to common courtesy." He gave DeKok another penetrating look. "By the way," he asked, "where's Vledder? He wasn't here, this morning."

DeKok rose from his chair and stared somberly at nothing at all. He did not answer. He wanted to spare the old man an outburst of anger. He really did not dislike his chief. Regardless of the many differences of opinion, he actually liked the old man.

"Where *is* Vledder?" repeated the Commissaris. His voice was suspicious.

DeKok swallowed.

"He . . . eh, he's gone to Seadike."

"WHAT!?"

DeKok slinked from the room. From a distance he could still hear the tirade of the Commissaris, although he had closed the door of the office behind him.

* * *

DeKok would have been surprised if he had seen the gently smiling face of the Commissaris at that moment. DeKok might be a master at manipulating people, but that did not mean that Commissaris had reached his present, exalted rank without being able to do his fair share of manipulating himself.

True, the Chief was constantly irritated with DeKok's irreverent attitude to authority. But he was also keenly aware that DeKok was the most successful detective on the force. He *always* solved his cases. Sometimes he did not solve them to the satisfaction of all concerned, especially that of the Judge-Advocate, or higher authority, but solve them he did. The old sleuth knew all the tricks and all the short-cuts, had thousands of contacts in the underworld, was able to insinuate his particular brand of logic into the most bizarre situations and, above all, was very, very effective.

His appearance was more often than not that of a country bumpkin in unfashionable clothes, an old raincoat or duffel coat, and his ever present, greasy, decrepit, little felt hat, grey hair peeking from under it in great, disordered tufts. He and Vledder made an excellent team. The old curmudgeon, tempered by years on the force into accepting the possible and the young, eager, well educated and sometimes impetuous Vledder, always striving for the impossible. The old and the new. The old hands-on cop and the new breed of policeman, college educated, technically inclined and with a high regard for rules and regulations.

The Commissaris had long since given up the hope that DeKok would ever be reconciled to the modern world. But he hoped fervently that, in time, Vledder would pick up some of DeKok's irreverence and brilliance. With Vledder's background and education, coupled with DeKok's experience and wisdom, Vledder might go far. He might become a Commissaris, maybe even Chief Constable.

* * *

Blissfully unaware of these thoughts, Inspector DeKok took the hefty file on Pete Geffel from a desk drawer, tucked it under one arm and disappeared into one of the interrogation rooms. He locked the door from the inside. He was consciously trying to avoid another confrontation with his angry chief. He did not feel like explaining Vledder's trip to Seadike. He would tell the old man when he was in a better, a more receptive mood.

While idly flipping the pages in the voluminous file, his thoughts wandered toward the beautiful and emotional Flossie. Obviously she was from a better, at least a more affluent environment than Cunning Pete. She was also, just as obviously, better educated than most. He reflected on her relationship with the glib, but superficial Pete Geffel, a man with an impressive string of arrests and convictions for his relatively young age. Women were marvelous creatures, he thought. They were almost always on the look-out for men they could 'reform', make over, change, whatever. It seemed, so thought DeKok, a natural trait. The only difference seemed strictly a matter of personal preference, whether the reform was for better, or worse. A man, he thought cynically, never knew what sort of woman would get a hold over him, would want to change him. But apparently Pete had fallen into good hands. Too late?

How stron had been Flossie's influence over him? Was she indeed the nice, kind girl to whom Pete had been devoted? And what was the meaning of that in connection with everything else? Musing on these and other questions, he was suddenly disturbed by a loud banging on the door of the small interrogation room. Vledder had returned from Seadike and demanded noisy admittance.

* * *

"What did you find out?"

Vledder pulled a sour face.

"It was mainly a disappointment. I don't have a lot of news for you. Almost everything known about Pete's murder *was* mentioned in the fax, yesterday morning. There simply were no usable technical details. Even the tire tracks were ordinary. I did make copies of all the reports that have been filed so far. But there seems to be no logical connection."

DeKok nodded thoughtfully.

"What about the official cause of death?"

"Post-mortem was this morning at ten. They were already working on it when I arrived. I waited for the results, such as they were, and interviewed Dr. Rusteloos. He was pretty positive, you know how he is. He had personally removed the dagger from the body. It was a narrow blade, but almost eight inches long. It had penetrated the body to the hilt. Upon further investigation, Dr. Rusteloos concluded that the wound must almost certainly have caused the death of the victim. The weapon had penetrated one of the lungs and the upper left chamber of the heart."

Pensively DeKok pulled on his lower lip.

"Almost eight inches . . . quite a bit."

Vledder nodded agreement.

"I've never seen a dagger like that before. It looked like an antique Italian *poniard*. Nice handwork on the silver handle, the grip, I mean."

"Are they doing anything with it, in Seadike?"

"Yes, they made pictures for circulation. They also want to check with antique dealers. It's a special weapon, possibly antique, as I said."

"Was there any mention about press, or TV?"

"Not that I know of. They'll probably wait until they've checked everything else."

Constable Bever entered the interrogation room at that moment. He had a folder under his arm. His face looked gray and his jovial expression was obscured by a worried look.

"Here's my report," he said dejectedly. "I had to re-write it four times." He snorted. "One thing is for sure. I'll never, ever shoot again. As far as I'm concerned they can have my pistol right now. Boy, oh, boy, what a trouble over two shots. Everybody is after your ass, the Inspector, the Chief-Inspector, the Commissaris, people from Internal Investigation, Headquarters, you name it. Couldn't you have done this? Or couldn't you have done that? Didn't you think it irresponsible to shoot in the street? After all, it's a bit risky, you know constable, you could have hit an innocent bystander. Did you think about that? Did you think about this? You never know what happens to the ricochet, you know. What if there had been a woman in the way, or a baby, would you still have used your pistol? . . ."

He slammed the report in front of Dekok, interrupting his Jeremiad.

"Dammit," he continued, "What in *hell* do they want from me? After all, you have to make a split decision and you do that, right?" He snorted again, managing to sound both indignant and sad. "After all," he concluded, "in a situation like that you simply don't have *time* to weigh all the consequences."

DeKok smiled a winning smile.

"Three million makes people nervous," he remarked cryptically.

Bever put a hand in a pocket of his uniform coat.

"Here's a letter for you," he growled, unwilling to listen to reason. "It was left with the desk-sergeant."

"Thank you."

Bever turned around and walked away without another word.

DeKok looked after him.

Constable Bever had grown years older in a single day.

Vledder picked up the letter and sniffed.

"Perfume," he established. He laughed at DeKok.

"I'm not surprised," he teased, "I bet it's from a beautiful blonde."

DeKok ignored the remark. He took the letter in his hands, pulled a small pocket knife from a pocket and opened the envelope. After having read the note from beginning to end, he repeated it out loud for Vledder's benefit.

Dear Mr. DeKok:
Thank you very much for your help. Our conversation has opened my eyes.
I now know what I have to do. You'll hear from me.
Flossie

Vledder frowned.

"Flossie . . . Flossie? Didn't Mother Geffel mention a Flossie, last night? Isn't that Pete's girlfriend?"

"Indeed."

"And you talked to her?"

"Indeed."

"When?"

"Last night, or rather, early this morning. After I took you home, I found her waiting for me outside the station house. I must say, it was an interesting conversation."

"Oh, yes?"

"Yes. Flossie, or as she's generally known more formally, Florentine La Croix, told me that she had loved her Peter very much. She was convinced that the feelings were reciprocated. In any case, they had no secrets from each other. Flossie knew about the robbery. Peter had explained it very nicely to her and, in passing, also told her how his knowledge could be transformed into cold, hard cash."

"As we suspected, blackmail?"

"Exactly."

"But Cunning Pete wasn't cunning enough. He was killed before he could put his plan into effect."

DeKok pulled on his lower lip and let it plop back. He repeated the annoying gesture several times. Finally he said:

"Yes, it seems that way. But it isn't at all certain that Pete was going to execute his blackmail plans. Flossie, you see, had overwhelming objections. She had taken it into her sweet head that Pete was going to change his life, was going to follow the narrow path of righteousness. She made him promise her to forget all about blackmail and to warn B&G of the intended hold-up."

Vledder's mouth fell open in utter astonishment.

"Warn B&G?"

"Yes, Pete was to call the company and inform them about the place and the time of the intended hold-up."

Vledder grinned.

"Of course, he didn't do that. That's obvious. Otherwise the company would have taken steps to prevent it from happening."

DeKok rubbed his hand through his gray hair.

"That, ... eh, that," he hesitated, "was also Flossie's opinion. She felt betrayed by her Peter and was very sad about it."

Vledder looked at him pensively, a suspicious glimmer in his eyes. He had heard a strange tone in DeKok's voice. A warning not to draw any hasty conclusions. Suddenly he took the letter from the table and read it several times from beginning to end. Then he looked at his mentor.

"You," he said slowly, almost accusingly, "you think that Pete Geffel *did* call in, after all."

8

Inspector Vledder was deep in thought.

It was very obvious. His face was tense. The square jaw with the dimple at the end of the chin pushed forward and there was a deep, diagonal crease between his eyebrows. Suddenly his eyes lit up. The chin was withdrawn and the frown disappeared.

"Eureka!" he exclaimed, "I've got it!"

DeKok looked up in surprise.

"What have you got?"

"I now know exactly what happened."

"Oh, yes?"

"Yes, everything . . . the entire plan."

"But, Dick, that's excellent, really excellent," mocked Dekok. "Then the whole case is solved."

Vledder did not react to the remark, nor to the mocking tone of voice. He moved his chair a bit closer to the table.

"Let us assume," he began, sticking a finger in the air in a subconscious imitation of one of DeKok's many mannerisms. "Let us assume," he continued, "that Pete, as you suspect, did indeed warn someone at B&G."

"Yes?"

"Therefore B&G *knew* that a robbery was planned."

"Of course."

"Well, what does B&G do then?"

"You tell me," was the laconic invitation.

"B&G," continued Vledder blithely, "doesn't lift a finger to stop the hold-up."

"Oh?"

"Yes, they don't lift a finger. They let it happen, including all the paperwork, the freight manifests, the works. The transport is just listed as one more transport. As a matter of fact, they take special pains to include a large amount of cash."

Vledder paused to gauge the effect of his statement.

"But . . . eh," he went on, "now comes the cute part: it's all just on paper. In reality the total sum is much, much smaller."

"Well, and?"

"Well, it's simple really. The difference between the recorded amount and the transported amount is pure profit because the insurance company will reimburse the loss." Vledder looked at his mentor with pride. "What do you think?" he asked.

DeKok nodded, deep in thought.

"It's possible . . ."

The younger man's eyes sparkled with an inner fire.

"Just think, DeKok, what genius! If the hold-up succeeds, the robbers will simply assume that they were unlucky and happened to hold up a particularly small transport. If, later, they read in the papers that the haul was supposedly much larger, they will simply dismiss it as just one more stunt from the police, just to create trouble in their ranks. But, of course they'd be forced to keep their mouth shut. Even if the hold-up did not succeed, or if something were to go wrong, nothing would be the matter. B&G would just apologize to their clients for a miscalculation, or they could simply announce that the Company had received an anonymous tip about a planned hold-up and they had taken the precaution to send less cash. The difference would, of course, be delivered at once. A most reasonable excuse."

DeKok smiled at his pupil, colleague and friend.

"Fantastic, Dick, simply fantastic." There was genuine admiration in his voice. "The plan does indeed border on genius. The logical way in which you explain it, is also pure genius. So simple, so straight-forward. At first hand, I don't have any arguments against it. I mean, I wouldn't be at all surprised if the plan really had been put together that way, the way you see it. It would also explain the murder in Seadike."

Vledder frowned.

"How's that?"

"For the plan to succeed, Pete had to disappear. There was no other choice."

Vledder sighed.

"I don't see that. I don't think the murder was essential. It increased the risks."

DeKok shook his head.

"No, no, not true. The murder safeguarded the plan. After all, Pete Geffel was the only one who could afterward testify that B&G was informed of the hold-up. A simple message to the insurance company would be enough to stop payment of damages. Let's not even mention, at this time, the possibility of Pete informing the police." He paused. "And after all, looked at objectively, was the risk of the murderer all that great? It would safeguard the plan. The plan itself was fool-proof. Just think, we only discovered the possible connection by accident."

Vledder nodded slowly.

"You're right, from their point of view it was better to silence Pete permanently."

DeKok rose with a sigh.

"Of course, we cannot be sure, but if it really happened the way we suspect, then it's a sad story, indeed." His voice sounded depressed. "Just think, the first time that Pete attempts to change his life, reform, if you will, the first time he turned his back on blackmail, on being a con-man, a petty thief, it becomes the direct cause of his death." Slowly he shook his head. "It could be a Greek drama," he concluded.

Vledder pressed his lips together.

"I know nothing about Greek dramas," he said, obviously irked. "Greek dramas don't interest me. I only know that it won't be easy to prove our suspicions."

DeKok grinned, a bit maliciously.

"In order words . . . you don't think we'll succeed. Well, one thing is for sure, the entire management of B&G will close ranks, silent ranks, against us." DeKok rubbed the bridge of his nose with a little finger. "And yet," he added, "that's also their weakness."

Vledder looked at him with surprise.

"Weakness?"

DeKok nodded.

"Think about the murder. We theorized that Pete Geffel was killed for the benefit of a certain group of people. But the actual act, you see, almost certainly was perpetrated by a single person, a man . . . or a woman. Therefore, you understand, one of the members of the group carries a heavier burden . . . is more vulnerable in relation to the remaining members of the group."

"I understand," admitted Vledder contemplatively. "The fact that *one* of them committed a murder, is also their weakness."

DeKok looked morosely at nothing at all.

"Except . . . except if they hired a killer between them. Somebody to do the dirty work, so to speak. But I find that hard to believe. The murder in Seadike doesn't smell like the work of a professional. Cunning Pete was a very smart sort of guy, streetwise, a blackmailer, an accomplished con-man. He knew people." He shook his head and sighed deeply. "*Cunning* Pete wasn't the sort of man who could be easily approached by a professional killer. He was too smart for that. No, considering the circumstances, there *had* to be some sort of association. I think, I don't know why, but I think that Pete *knew* his killer . . . must have trusted him, or her, right up to the last moment." He paused. "And remember, you have to consider that the group had little time," he added.

"How's that?"

"Well, the time for preparation was short. Just think! B&G couldn't do a thing until *after* they had been informed about the plans for a hold-up. Only then could they begin to plan their counter-moves. In reality the time must have been even shorter, because I assume that it took some time before they could evaluate all the possibilities and consequences. The plan must have grown slowly, must have been subject to consideration, and finally approved and executed. That leaves very little time to search for, find and hire a professional killer. After all, you don't select one from the Yellow Pages." He grinned lop-sidedly at the bitter jest. "No, Dick," he continued, shaking his head, "not a professional killer, but a very cold-blooded amateur. As far as I'm concerned, the killer can be found among top management of B&G."

Vledder looked grave. His fists were balled in his pockets and there was a determined look on his face.

"Dammit, DeKok," he exclaimed vehemently, "we *must* find Pete Geffel's killer! We must! It's no more than our duty. Not just because of our job, our prestige, or for justice, or whatever, but . . ."

He did not complete the sentence.

DeKok looked at him searchingly.

"What are you trying to say, Dick?"

Vledder swallowed, then he spoke reluctantly:

"We . . . eh, we owe it to an innocent blackmailer."

* * *

It was raining.

DeKok had pulled up the collar of his coat. The miserable, depressing weather made him melancholy. His moods were as predictable as a barometer. A deep depression in the weather front, could be read off his face.

He looked sideways at Vledder who was walking next to him. The boy improved by the day, he thought. His powers of deduction had shown considerable progress and his self-confidence was markedly better. And especially the last, was of prime importance to a beginning policeman. The solution of crimes was not merely a matter of sharpness. Perseverance and a belief in oneself were the most important weapons in the battle against crime.

He grinned silently to himself.

But usually, more often than he cared to admit, a little bit of luck was the deciding factor in coming to a satisfactory conclusion. His thoughts drifted toward B&G. He had been on the job more than twenty five years, but had never before encountered quite such a dangerous opponent. He wondered if Vledder and he were right to tackle them head-on. Perhaps they were getting careless and overconfident.

He thought about Pete Geffel and his lonely death in the sand dunes and suddenly, in the middle of the street, he stopped. Deep wrinkles had formed in his forehead and there was a pensive look in his eyes.

Vledder who had progressed several paces beyond, stopped also and turned with an expression of surprise on his face.

"What's the matter?"

DeKok wiped the rain from his face.

"What did Pete do, to warn them?"

Vledder grinned in reply.

"He phoned."

"And who answered the telephone?"

The young inspector shrugged his shoulders.

"Most likely a receptionist."

For a long time DeKok chewed thoughtfully on his lower lip. At moments like that he resembled a cow chewing its cud. Vledder watched the expression with a puzzled look on his face. On the New Fort Canal DeKok entered the offices of the "Amsterdam Times" and asked the doorman to use the phone. Vledder smiled. Walkie-talkies and radios did not belong with DeKok's concepts of communication methods.

The doorman, who had known DeKok for years, readily assented. DeKok disappeared in the tiny space where the doorman kept a phone, his logbook and a number of telephone directories.

He looked for the phone number of B&G. He was convinced that Pete would have followed the same method.

When he found the number, he picked up the receiver and dialed the number. With a certain satisfaction a subconscious part of his mind approved of the old-fashioned dial on the phone. DeKok did not like touch phones, either. After a few rings a female voice answered at the other end.

"With B&G, how may I help you?"

DeKok swallowed. Hastily disguising his voice, he said:

"I ... eh, I ... have an important message. Very important. I want to talk to ... eh, the top man."

"What is this about?"

"A hold-up ... a hold-up on a transport."

There was a pause at the other end of the line.

"I'll connect you."

It took several seconds. Then there was some crackling on the line and a male voice answered:

"Thornbush ... who is this? Hello ... who's calling? Hello ..."

DeKok did not answer. Carefully he replaced the receiver.

9

"I refuse."

President Bent pushed himself abruptly forward in his easy chair and slapped his knee with the palm of his hand. His aristocratic face was red with indignation.

"I refuse to assemble management for your convenience to . . . to . . . eh, to line them up, as if they were a bunch of criminals."

DeKok looked at him for a long time. There was a playful smile around his lips.

"That's *your* interpretation, Mr. Bent," he said sarcastically. "I wouldn't dream of calling your eminent staff a bunch of criminals."

Agitated, the president rose from his chair.

"You know very well what I mean," he hissed vehemently. "If you ask me to assemble for you all the people who knew about the size of that particular transport, then there is only one possible explanation . . ."

DeKok looked at him evenly.

"Is that so?"

Bent sighed deeply.

"Really, seriously, Inspector!" He sounded desperate, trying to control himself. "You're on the wrong track with your investigation. I don't understand your stubborn attitude. After all, I take it that your Commissaris has given you specific instructions?"

DeKok nodded.

"Indeed," he said. "The Commissaris told me to investigate the hold-up and he said to be nice to Mr. Bent. I'm not to say nasty things to you. According to the Commissaris, you have tender feelings and are easily hurt."

Vledder supported his colleague.

"And we *will* take your soft, kind character into consideration, Mr. Bent. But . . . that's the only concession we can make."

Bent's face became even redder. It did not seem possible.

"I don't need your concessions" he screamed angrily. "But I'll be damned before I lend my cooperation to chasing a mirage. I repeat: The solution is not to be found with me, or within the Company. Put that out of your head! Believe me, you're chasing rainbows, specters." He was close to losing control again.

The expression on DeKok's friendly, melancholy face changed into an even, expressionless, implacable mask.

"Rainbows? Specters?" he asked softly, but threateningly. His voice sounded like the voice of doom. "Mr. Bent, we're not chasing specters, but a phantom, just *one* phantom . . . the phantom of a murderer." Vledder admired the lugubrious sounds DeKok was able to produce.

The president fell back in his chair, apparently deflated.

"A murderer?"

DeKok gauged the amount of surprise on Bent's face. He wondered how much was real and how much was well-played innocence. It was almost too good to be true, the bulging eyes, the half-open mouth.

He nodded.

"Yes, the man, or woman, who killed Pete Geffel."

Bent was a picture of incomprehension.

"Who ... who is Pete Geffel?"

"The man," answered DeKok slowly, "who called B&G last week to alert you about a possible hold-up."

Bent stared at him dumbfounded. All intelligence seemed to have left his face.

"W-what ... what?" he stammered.

DeKok looked at him evenly.

"You heard me, Mr. Bent." There was icy sarcasm in his voice. "Pete Geffel called last week to warn you about a hold-up that had been planned for one of your transports. He wanted to clear his conscience and, at the same time, protect you from a great financial loss. It was his death. Somebody enticed him into the sand dunes near Seadike and planted a dagger in his back." He paused, gauged the reaction. "Now do you understand, Mr. Bent, why I have such an insatiable curiosity about that ... eh, that bunch of criminals of yours?"

Mr. Bent shielded his eyes with his left hand. The other hand, resting loosely on the armrest of the chair, shook lightly. It took a long time before he answered.

"I must assume," he said hoarsely, "that you know what you're talking about. I mean, that your information is correct. You see, if the message of ... eh, Pete Geffel you said? If Geffel's message had reached us in time, we would most certainly have taken steps."

DeKok made a vague gesture.

"Indeed, that's exactly what puzzles us as well. I mean, at the very least a company like B&G can be expected to protect its assets."

Bent nodded slowly.

"I understand what you're thinking. No measures were taken. Our company took no steps to prevent the loss. Despite the warning, the hold-up took place as planned."

"Exactly! Not even the police were informed. And I can't help but wonder: WHY? What could the company possibly gain by doing nothing?"

Sighing deeply, Bent rose from his chair.

"I won't fight you any longer, Mr. DeKok. I realize that it would be counter-productive."

He walked over to the desk and pushed a button.

"Tell Thornbush to come in here." His voice sounded wan, without strength. The president was the epitome of a tired man. His eyes were dull and his face was gray. All inner strength seemed to have been sapped from his body. "Thornbush is our Vice President of Administration," he explained to the policemen.

A man entered after a few seconds. He stopped in the middle of the room. Nervously, he looked around.

DeKok looked at him intently. He was a relatively young man, a southern type with shiny, black hair and somewhat weak facial structure. He wore a stylish corn-flower blue suit with expensive shoes. He made a foppish impression on DeKok's puritanical soul.

Bent gestured.

"These gentlemen are Inspectors DeKok and Vledder from the Warmoes Street Station. They have been assigned to the hold-up case. I have just told them that they have the 'freedom of the office' and that there will be no restrictions on the questions they may ask our personnel. They can ask what they want, from who they want, regardless of position. I would like you to take care of all formalities and make sure that their every wish will be obeyed." He turned to DeKok with a small bow. "Satisfied?" It sounded sarcastic.

DeKok gave him a friendly grin.

"Completely."

"Then, will you excuse me?"

Head down, Bent left the office with a reluctant, hesitating step. The door slammed closed behind him.

* * *

DeKok had tired feet.

With a painful expression he lifted his legs and placed them on top of the desk. It was if a thousand devils pushed red-hot needles into his calves. When it happened it was always a bad sign. And sometimes it happened too often. Whenever a case seemed to progress slowly, or in the wrong direction, when he had the feeling he was drifting farther and farther away from a solution, then he felt his feet, his tired feet and that is when the little devils played their sadistic little games with his lower extremities.

And things had not gone well. The visit to the offices of B&G had not produced any tangible results. As expected, the top management of B&G formed ranks against the intruder. They displayed a united picture of pure innocence and he had not been able to crack the facade. In a circumspect way he had mentioned Pete Geffel. He had left no doubt in their minds about his opinion about murder and he had hinted about the possible perpetrator. The gentlemen had listened politely to his statements, had smiled starchy smiles and that had been their only reaction.

Eventually he had felt that perhaps Bent was right and that he was barking up the wrong tree at B&G.

Across his wide shoes with the painful, flat feet, he looked at Vledder who was working on one of his interminable reports.

"Are you about finished, Dick? I mean, do you have a list of all the people who knew about the amount to be transported?"

"Vledder nodded.

"Oh, yes. I've got that."

"Read it to me."

The young inspector picked up his notes and walked over to DeKok's desk.

"Well," he sighed. "At the top of the list is the President, Bent and . . ."

"A man," interrupted DeKok, "about whom it is said that he should not have married for the second time."

"Then there is the Executive Vice President, Bergen," continued Vledder.

DeKok nodded slowly.

"The man from Haarlem, who, coincidentally owns a blue Simca that, just as coincidentally, was stolen and used for the hold-up."

"Then there's Bakelsma, the Vice President of Finance and two more Vice Presidents, Meeden and Westfall."

DeKok made a helpless gesture.

"All people who are the very picture of reliability and trustworthiness, no doubt."

Vledder grinned.

"And finally, the Secretary of the organization, also the Vice President of Administration, Thornbush."

DeKok lifted his legs from the desk.

"The only man, by the way, who doesn't seem to fit in the overall picture. He's different."

Vledder grinned maliciously.

"Oh, come now, just because he dresses a little snappier than the rest, doesn't make him a criminal." The tone was sarcastic, as if the young inspector did not believe his own statement.

DeKok looked at him.

"But you forget, that he's the man who probably received Pete's telephonic warning. It's exceedingly strange, however, that none of the receptionists can remember such a call coming through during the time *before* the hold-up. There must, of course, have been a number of calls on the subject *after* the hold-up. Then again, at best they would hear snatches of conversations. I don't think they would purposely listen in."

Vledder gestured.

"That can mean one of two things: Geffel never called, or, if he did call, he asked for somebody in particular. Maybe he knew somebody's name, one way or the other. But in either case, it would be unlikely that a receptionist would remember any details of a call that was made more than a week ago. Also, I doubt that Pete mentioned his name."

DeKok nodded reflectively.

"There is a third possibility."

Vledder looked the question.

"The particular receptionist has been well instructed."

Vledder frowned.

"You mean she *does* remember the conversation, but somebody instructed her to keep her mouth shut?"

"Exactly."

Vledder shook his head dejectedly.

"It's a hopeless situation," he said bleakly. "We'll never get anywhere this way. The circle of suspects and accessories becomes wider and wider."

For a long time both remained silent, thinking their own thoughts.

DeKok stood up and walked over to the window. He placed himself in his favorite position, balancing on the balls of his feet, his hands folded behind his back. He stared out of the window at the rooftops across the street. A light snow fall had transformed the rooftops and chimneys under the gray skies into an idealized version of a Christmas postcard. After a long while he turned around.

"You know, Dick," he said slowly, choosing his words, "we are forgetting, I think, that the hold-up actually *did* take place. We seem to have forgotten that, neglected it, rather."

Vledder looked at him in surprise.

"I don't understand you."

"Well, it's simple, really. Who committed the robbery? Although B&G probably, according to our theory, took advantage of the information provided by Pete, there were actual people involved in the hold-up. Real people who really *did* commit the crime."

Vledder nodded.

"Of course, but I don't think that those people are in any way connected with B&G. They probably also have nothing to do with Pete's killing."

DeKok smiled.

"But they are in a position to provide us with proof about that."

"Proof?"

"Yes, if we can arrest the robbers and if they can prove that the haul was considerably less than reported by B&G . . ."

Vledder's eyes sparkled.

" ... then," he interrupted enthusiastically, "then we could really put the screws to B&G management."

"Yes, indeed. It would help us considerably. Perhaps we can get one of them to talk."

Vledder's face fell.

"Well, yes, that would be great, but how do we find the perpetrators? I mean, we can hardly place an ad in the papers, now can we?"

DeKok laughed at him.

"Don't be so pessimistic. After all, we are policemen, you know. I'm sure we can solve it. To begin with, here's an intriguing question for you."

"Question?"

DeKok nodded indulgently.

"Yes. How did Pete Geffel know that a hold-up was in the making?"

For several seconds Vledder was dumbfounded. Then he covered his face in his hands and groaned.

"Of course," he exclaimed, "of course. I never gave it a thought. He *had* to hear it from somebody."

DeKok rubbed his face with both hands. It was a tired gesture.

"And he had been well informed. He knew exactly what was going to happen. Therefore, I think he got his information first hand."

Vledder looked at him searchingly.

"You mean, he got his information directly from one of the robbers?"

DeKok placed a fatherly hand on the broad shoulders of the younger man.

"It seems that way. And if I then tell you that Pete had been out of jail for less than a month, according to his file,

101

and that he had spent the last few months of his jail sentence in Haarlem, what would be your conclusion?"

The expression on Vledder's face became noticeably more cheerful.

"That Geffel gained his knowledge in jail."

DeKok nodded encouragingly.

"Exactly. Therefore I think you should make another trip to Haarlem. Have a talk with the warden there. He would be able to tell you who shared a cell with Pete."

"Then what?"

"Then you come back to the station. Don't try any arrests on your own."

"And what will you be doing?"

DeKok looked into the distance without seeing anything.

"I promised myself a long conversation with Flossie."

"Flossie?"

DeKok nodded slowly.

"Yes. I'm afraid she has an ulterior motive. You see, this afternoon I spotted her in one of the corridors at B&G."

10

With his collar pulled up high, his hands deep in his pockets and his little, decrepit felt hat far back on his head, DeKok stared across the Brewers Canal. Florentine La Croix lived just across the inky waters, near the corner of Pilgrim Street.

He had seen her enter more than half an hour ago, accompanied by a young man and he wondered how much longer the visit was likely to last. To be honest, he had no inclination to remain much longer on the drafty, cold corner in the hope that the young man would soon take his leave.

He grinned quietly to himself. Perhaps he intended to stay the night and had no plans of leaving at all. You never knew with women. One moment they seemed broken in body and spirit because of the loss of a loved one and the next moment they had cheerfully engaged in a new relationship. Come to think of it, reflected DeKok, the same could be said for almost anybody. People were wonderful.

He scratched the back of his neck. Women and love, he thought, returning to his original thought, he could not help it. They were factors he always looked at with a certain amount of suspicion. Perhaps it was because he did not understand women. What man could? But it seemed as if their capricious characters had confronted him with many a surprise on several occasions during his long career as a cop. And DeKok did not really like surprises. He preferred to work within the trusted framework of a regular routine. Surprises worried him. Yet, he relished the challenge of every new mystery. Sometimes, thought DeKok ruefully, I am too complicated for my own good.

He looked at his watch and decided to allow the young man another fifteen minutes. When the allotted time had past, he ambled away from his post, crossed the narrow bridge toward the other side of the canal and approached the corner of Pilgrim Street. Meanwhile he searched in his pocket for the invaluable gadget that had so often allowed him to open doors that seemed impenetrable. The gadget had been a gift from Handy Henkie, a reformed burglar. DeKok would not readily be without it and this time too, he silently thanked Henkie for his invention.

Without any trouble at all, he opened the front door and then he carefully hoisted his two hundred pounds up the narrow, creaking stairs. He paused in the corridor on the second floor. The building was one of those typical Amsterdam canal houses. Three floors, each with their own entrance into what had once been a single family residence. But that was several centuries ago. The exploding population and the price of real estate had forced many subdivisions of this kind. Few people could still afford a large house like this just for themselves. Certainly not in the city. Apparently this particular floor was subdivided again. The front of the house and the back area had both been rented to separate tenants.

He waited until he had his breath under control once again. With a smile he realized that he had held his breath while climbing the stairs. He carefully felt the knob of the front living room and when he ascertained that it was locked as well, he again fished Henkie's gadget from his pocket.

Cautiously he pushed the door until it was barely open. He heard the murmur of voices. A man and a woman spoke in turns. But no matter how he strained his ears, he could not distinguish any words or sentences in the series of sounds that reached him. He hesitated for just one more moment, then he entered.

His sudden appearance in the living room caused a certain amount of commotion. The young man hastily rose from an easy chair and looked at DeKok with large, surprised eyes. His long, gaunt face was pale and the corners of his mouth trembled.

Flossie, too, stood up. Blood rose to her head and her face became a deep red. Anger flashed in her bright, blue eyes. With an abrupt gesture she tossed her long, blonde hair backward.

"What ... eh? How ... eh?"

Apparently she was unable to formulate her questions in a coherent manner.

With a shy smile on his face, DeKok stood in the middle of the room. His hat in his hand. He made a bumbling gesture toward the door.

"Please excuse me. I ... eh, I knocked several times," he lied. "But nobody heard me, it seems. And because the door was ajar, I just came in."

She looked at him with suspicion.

"The door was locked," she declared firmly.

DeKok shrugged his shoulders. He thought it better to ignore the subject. The young man obviously felt ill at ease.

"I ... eh, maybe I better leave," he whispered.

She gave him a sweet smile.

"All right, Frits, go on. We'll see each other tomorrow. I'm sorry," she continued, with a vague gesture toward DeKok, "I had no idea that Uncle would arrive today."

The young man grabbed his coat from a nearby chair, stammered a greeting and left hastily. Flossie and DeKok watched him leave. They heard him stumble on the stairs.

When the front door had closed behind him, DeKok unbuttoned his coat and nestled himself comfortably in one of the easy chairs.

Still standing, Flossie looked down on him. Her long, shapely legs spread, her hands on her hips in a challenging stance.

"Intruder," she hissed. "You don't fool me. The door was locked!"

DeKok grinned and despite herself she was momentarily charmed by the boyish jollity that transformed his face.

"Let's not make a federal case out of it," he replied airily. "I just didn't feel like waiting until the young man had left. That's all."

Confused, she looked at him.

"But how did you . . ."

DeKok waved her question away.

"Forget it, Flossie. I've got my little secrets." He smiled. "Why don't you make your dear uncle a nice cup of coffee. Because *Uncle* isn't about to leave anytime soon." His emphasis on the word "uncle" suddenly reminded her that it was Amsterdam slang for a police constable, one of the few slang words that could be directly traced. Shortly after the Nazi Occupation, some genius, in an attempt to make youth less afraid of people in uniform, had started a campaign promoting "Uncle Police".

"Uncle has a lot of things to discuss with you," added DeKok.

"Oh, cut out the 'uncle' stuff," she snapped. "After all, I could hardly tell that boy you're a cop."

DeKok grinned broadly.

"But why not? It's an honorable profession."

Moodily she shrugged her shoulders.

"I didn't want him to know who you were." She paused. "Besides," she continued after a while, "it would spoil my plans."

DeKok looked at her searchingly.

"Plans?"

She did not answer. Slowly she turned around and walked toward the alcove that had been fitted out as a kitchen. She returned into the living room after a few seconds.

"You know all about my plans," she said.

DeKok sighed.

"You mean, of course, your plans regarding Pete's killer."

Her face became serious.

"I'll find him." She stared past him at nothing in particular. Her big, cornflower-blue eyes had a strange shine, almost otherworldly. "I'll find him," she repeated tonelessly. "I'll find him before *you* do."

DeKok looked at her until the strange gleam had left her eyes.

"Is that . . . ," he asked carefully, "why you invited that young man here?"

She did not answer. She smoothed her skirt with a routine gesture and sank down into one of the chairs. Her challenging, obstreperous attitude had disappeared.

"Why did you invite . . . Frits, was it? Why did you invite him over?"

"He's from the office."

"The B&G office?"

"Yes."

"How did you get to know him?"

"I work there."

"What?"

She smiled faintly.

"Last night, after our conversation, I realized that the murderer had to be found at B&G. I laid awake all night. The more I thought about it, the surer I was. That's when I wrote you the note." She sighed deeply. "This morning I went to the office at the Emperor's Canal and asked if there were any openings. I'm an excellent typist, you know."

"And?"

"I was hired on the spot."

DeKok pressed his lips together.

"And then you immediately found this young man, Frits, played up to him, perhaps, all in order to learn more about the internal relationships at B&G?"

"Yes."

Bemused, DeKok shook his head.

"But don't you understand," he said earnestly, "that you're playing a very dangerous game? If the killer really works at B&G and if he discovers, no matter how, *who* you are and what you're after . . ." He did not complete the sentence. "Did you really think that the man, or woman . . . whatever, would hesitate about a second murder?"

The kettle started to whistle in the alcove. Without answering she stood up and attended to it. She returned a little later with two steaming mugs of coffee.

DeKok watched her closely. She was completely calm. With a steady hand she placed the mugs on a small table. She seemed a different woman. He could not find anything in her demeanor that reminded him of the scared, emotional being who had waited for him the night before. Her face looked very serious and there was a determined expression around her mouth. Even her beauty seemed to have chilled, as if an icy wind had blown away all inner warmth. Ice Queen, thought DeKok.

She gave him a pitying look.

"I believe," she said softly, "that you don't understand at all."

DeKok rubbed his gray hair in a despairing gesture.

"No," he sighed. "I've always had trouble comprehending the turmoils of the soul. Especially those of beautiful women. It's really too bad that I so often seem to be confronted with them. I guess it's fate."

A big, black tomcat rose lazily from a spot near the fireplace. It sniffed DeKok's trouser legs disdainfully and then jumped lightly on Flossie's lap.

"I'm not afraid of danger," she said, softly stroking the cat. "I *will* find Peter's killer, his murderer, and I'll accept the risks connected with that." A bitter smile marred her perfect lips. "And I will find him before he winds up in the weak, powerless hands of your so-called *justice*." She almost spat the last word with special emphasis and a considerable amount of contempt.

DeKok looked at her evenly.

"My justice, Flossie? What's my justice? I'm only a civil servant, a servant of the State. That's all."

Her blue eyes sparkled dangerously.

"Exactly," she exclaimed vehemently. "It's no business of the State. It's not *your* business. It's no business for the police. Don't you understand? It's not your concern. This is between me and whoever killed my Peter." She looked at him evenly. "And nobody else," she concluded.

DeKok shook his head.

"This is no child's play, Flossie, it's not a game of hide-and-seek. Leave that sinister office. The people who are responsible for the death of your Peter are cool, calculating people, who, when push comes to shove, are capable of anything. Believe me, you'll never succeed in unmasking the killer. You only run the risk of ending your life the way Peter did . . ."

She pressed her lips together.

"I don't care how my life ends. Don't you understand?" There was desperation in her voice. "I've got a debt to pay. Me, me with my narrow-minded morals, my naive ideas about good and evil . . . *I killed Peter!*" She paused, gathering her thoughts. "For days I nagged him, begged him . . . exploited his feelings for me . . . until he finally agreed to call the company. I drove him to his death." She took a few deep breaths, fought against the tears in her eyes. Then she continued:

"Peter . . . Peter lived off the gullibility of other people, their greed. He blackmailed them, he cheated them, he conned them. But was that so bad? I should have left well enough alone. I should have *let* him take the guys for the money. Then we could have married. Now, what do I have?" She made a sad gesture. The cat opened one eye. "I have dear parents, but they raised me the old-fashioned way. They told me that goodness, truth, is its own reward. Maybe they didn't know any better. But it was a lie . . . a lie . . . a lie . . ." She slammed her fist on one knee. The cat, vaguely alarmed, opened both eyes.

DeKok rubbed his face with a flat hand. He felt miserable. In order to cheer her up, to restore her faith in her Peter, he had told her, only last night, that her fiancé had not betrayed her and had really called in the warning. The intelligent girl, no doubt aided by a healthy amount of intuition, had drawn the obvious conclusion. Peter had been killed by somebody at B&G . . . and she blamed herself!

Pensively he looked at the young woman across from him. Her body was almost motionless, tense, with an inner tautness that was only evident from the hand that mechanically stroked the black tomcat in her lap. He full well realized that she was capable of almost anything in her present state of bitterness, even murder, and he hoped fervently that he would be able to find Pete Geffel's killer *before* he fell into *her* hands.

He looked at the fingers that stroked the cat. They were long and sinewy. The wrist and muscles of her forearm seemed more developed than was usual in a woman. Still graceful, but strong.

"I must warn you officially," he sighed, "not to take matters into your own hands. Don't do anything dumb. Peter is dead. That's irrevocable. Nothing . . . absolutely nothing can change that. And you can't live with the dead. Life is for the living." He scratched the back of his neck. Hating himself for the facile platitudes he was using. "It's useless, wasteful," he continued, "to waste your young life for an *idee fixe*, an obsession, a silly idea."

That got her attention.

"A silly idea?"

He nodded slowly.

"It's a silly idea to convince yourself that you're guilty of Peter's death. It's just silly."

She gave him a wan smile.

"Love and happiness . . . those are silly ideas, too. Ideas full of misunderstandings, mistakes. I know that." She shrugged her shoulders. "Yet, I'm prepared to do silly things because of those silly ideas."

DeKok swallowed. He understood that he had lost the battle. He had no arguments left. Florentine La Croix had taken the first steps on her path to vengeance.

She was determined. She would find the murderer of Peter Geffel and . . . she would punish him. She saw it as a holy task, a calling, and nobody was going to stop her. He made one last attempt.

"I offer you a partnership," he proposed seriously. "Let's find Peter's killer together. I . . . eh, I have *some* experience."

Slowly she shook her head.

"I don't need your help. When necessary, I'll call you to . . . to do your duty." There was a mocking tone in her voice.

DeKok lowered his head. Two mugs of coffee were sitting on the small table between them. Untouched.

After a few more seconds he rose slowly, buttoned his coat and murmured an inaudible goodbye. At the door he turned around once more. The tomcat on her lap seemed to give him a malicious grin.

11

A wad of chewing gum between his powerful jaws and with a gruff look on his face, DeKok walked across the narrow bridge across the Brewers Canal and from there, through the many alleys and along the maze of canals to Warmoes Street. He ignored the vague greetings and half smiles of the shady characters and prostitutes along the way. His thoughts were occupied by Flossie. Rebellious, defiant, vengeful Flossy. He understood what motivated her, of course, and he could even sympathize with her to a certain extent. But that was all. He certainly was not prepared to become her personal guardian angel. If she insisted on stepping into a hornet's nest, if she really wanted to track down Pete's killer all by herself, she could just go ahead.

With a sudden expression of disgust he spat out the wad of chewing gum. At times like this he longed for one of his cigars that he had long since given up. He had not smoked for years, but still the longing sometimes overpowered him. He always resisted it. He felt for another stick of gum and then decided against that as well. His thoughts returned to Flossie.

Her personal actions were no concern of his. Officially they were none of his business. He had enough on his plate as it was, even without Flossie trying to act as a detective. Who did she think she was, anyway. Solve the puzzle all by her lonesome, would she? He grinned at the thought. Stupid, silly business. With a last, half-hearted curse aimed at all beautiful, blonde women in the world, he entered the station house.

* * *

The desk sergeant emerged from his high bench as soon as he saw DeKok enter.

"Vledder left barely fifteen minutes ago."

DeKok looked at him with surprise.

"Where to? Didn't he go to Haarlem?"

"Oh, he's back from there already. He came in here about fifteen minutes ago and went straight on to Maltese Cross Alley. He's supposed to be waiting for you there, on the corner of Farmer's Alley."

"But why?"

The desk sergeant shrugged his shoulders.

"That's all he told me to tell you. It's all I know." He gave DeKok a reproachful look. "It's your own fault. Why don't you carry a walkie-talkie. Why do you always insist on walking? Hell, we can't even get you on the police radio. But then, you guys in plain clothes are always so secretive." He returned to his desk and sat down. Then he looked up. "Oh, yeah," he added, "a woman called you several times."

"A woman?"

"Yes."

"What's her name?"

"I don't know. I asked, but she wouldn't tell me. She just said that she *had* to speak to you, personally."

DeKok grinned.

"Oh, well," he said finally, resignation in his voice, "if it's important, she'll call again."

He waved at the sergeant and left the station.

* * *

As usual, it was busy in Warmoes Street and the area around it. The bars and night clubs were filled to overflowing. Groups of drunks staggered from one bar to the next and the Red Light District was operating at capacity. The curtains in front of the windows that indicated whether a room was "occupied" or not, opened and closed with the regularity of a well-oiled machine. A detachment of the British Fleet was in port and large contingents of British sailors searched avidly for sex, fun and pleasure. Amsterdam's Red Light District absorbed them all and tended to their needs, desires and lusts.

DeKok passed through it all with a nonchalance bred from familiarity. He knew the business of the Quarter, the fat madams, the smooth pimps, the suspicious characters, the beautiful, often exotic ladies of the "Life". The Quarter had no secrets for him. He thought about Vledder and wondered why his young colleague had so suddenly left for Farmer's Alley. He must have discovered something. But what could possibly be found in the Farmer's Alley, a decrepit, neglected passage-way in a dark corner of the District. It was, of course, typical of DeKok that he never once considered contacting Vledder via a walkie-talkie, although they had by now become so small and unobtrusive that he would hardly have noticed their presence. Also, despite the apparent urgency of the call, he walked. Anyway, he was convinced that the fastest way to get around the inner city of Amsterdam was either on foot, or on a bicycle. And he had not ridden a bicycle for years. Besides, however innocuous, a bicycle was a mechanical contraption. DeKok did not like modern means of communication and transportation, avoided them as much as possible.

With his typical, somewhat waddling gait, he crossed the Quarter, in one alley and out another, across some forgotten footbridge and along a deserted canal, places unknown even to many native Amsterdammers. Finally he turned the corner of Maltese Cross Alley, saw Farmer's Alley and the silhouette of Vledder. Softly he approached.

Vledder was visibly startled by his sudden, silent arrival.

"Damn," he whispered, "is it you?"

DeKok pulled a serious face.

"You're not very alert for a policeman," he admonished. "That could be fatal, one of these days. You should have seen me coming."

Vledder nodded silent assent.

"You're right," he allowed after a while. "It was stupid. I didn't watch that side at all. I was too occupied by the Alley."

DeKok nodded.

"What's in the Alley?"

"The hiding place of the gang."

"What!?"

Vledder grinned softly.

"Yes, the guys who robbed the transport were supposed to use an old, abandoned warehouse to lie low."

"Who told you that?"

"A prisoner in Haarlem."

DeKok's eyebrows danced briefly. Vledder thought he saw the remarkable phenomenon, but unfortunately it was too dark.

"And he just told you that?"

Vledder sighed elaborately.

"Well, I asked the warden who had associated with Geffel during his incarceration. There were quite a few."

"How's that?"

"Actually, you can't exclude anyone. After all, the prisoners meet each other in the work shops, on the exercise yards. Did you know they even have a swimming pool there? Anyway, Cunning Pete could have gotten the information from just about anybody in that prison."

"Very well, then what?"

"Well, I asked the warden to tell me who had been Pete's cell-mate during the last few months. This turned out to be an old guy called 'Uncle Safe'. It seems that 'Uncle Safe' is a rather old burglar who used to specialize in antique safes. I talked to him. At first he didn't want to tell me a thing, but after I told him that Pete was dead and how he had lost his life, he became more forthcoming. 'If you ever tell anyone I told you, I'll call you a liar to your face,' he said, 'but there's an old abandoned warehouse in Farmers Alley in Amsterdam. Go have a look there.' I tried to get him to tell me more, but he clammed up after that."

DeKok nodded pensively.

"And then you rushed right over to arrest the supposed gang." Vledder could almost taste the sarcastic tone of voice.

"Well, no ... eh, no, or rather, yes. I ... I didn't want to waste any time."

DeKok smiled.

"Did you know that Farmer's Alley makes a sharp turn a little further down and that there's another exit toward the Cleavers Canal? While you stood here, guarding one end of the alley, they could have left by the other side."

Blood rushed to Vledder's head.

"I thought it was a dead-end. Anyway," he continued, irritated, subconsciously contradicting himself, "I wasn't after an arrest. I knew very well that I couldn't do that by myself. I just wanted to take a look. That's all."

"And?"

"What?"

"Is there an old, abandoned warehouse?"

"Yes, just a little down the alley, on the left side. It has an entrance with double doors. They were opened recently. The hinges are oiled."

DeKok pushed his hat further back on his head.

"Excellent," he grinned, "really excellent. Then the doors won't squeak for us, either."

He felt for Handy Henkie's little gadget in his trouser pocket and stepped into the Alley. Vledder followed with a flashlight.

DeKok had little trouble with the ancient lock. His experienced fingers touched the lock, made some adjustments to the gadget and the lock softly clicked open. Softly he pushed the doors ajar. The hinges were as soundless as they had hoped. Vledder aimed his flashlight into the interior. A set of bright, green cat's eyes lit up like forgotten Christmas lights. As the two man carefully pushed the door wider, the animal slipped between their legs into the Alley. Nothing else moved. Carefully, following the cone of light as it explored the interior, they tiptoed into the warehouse. Slowly their eyes adjusted to the dark. They saw a number of empty racks and shelves. A thick layer of dust covered everything. Two doors were situated at the end of the main floor. One opened up on a filthy toilet, the other revealed a sparsely furnished room with black paper glued to the windows. DeKok found a switch. A few wires with a bare bulb hung from the ceiling. It illuminated a couple of dirty beds, an old sofa, three rickety chairs and a wooden table.

"We're too late," said Vledder regretfully. "The birds have flown the coup."

DeKok nodded.

"They *were* here." His gaze wandered through the room. He took it all in, recorded it like a movie camera. Every detail was imprinted in his brain. "In any case," he added carefully, "a number of men lived here for some time. I don't think they'll be back."

Vledder gave him a surprised look.

"Why not? After all, they can't know we have discovered their hideaway!"

DeKok rubbed an index finger across one of the backs of the chairs.

"Wiped clean," he remarked resignedly. "They didn't want to leave any fingerprints." He placed a pinky into the neck of an empty whiskey bottle on the table. Carefully he lifted the bottle and breathed on the glass. "You see, no prints."

Suddenly he noticed the label on the bottle, took a closer look and examined a small scratch near one edge. Carefully he replaced the bottle on the table. There was a faint smile around his lips.

Vledder rummaged around. In a corner of the room he leaned forward. He had found a set of old license tags. He picked them up and placed them on the table. Both plates showed the numbers NG-12-83. The young Inspector's eyes gleamed.

"The tags from the blue Simca," he said enthusiastically.

DeKok looked at the tags.

"You're right," he agreed. "They probably clamped them over the existing plates, there are some scratches on the edges. They removed them immediately after the hold-up"

Vledder gestured.

"But that would mean that the robbers must have been here very shortly after the hold-up. They may have come here directly. Apparently they thought it too dangerous to keep driving around with the false tags."

DeKok rubbed his face with both hands.

"I wonder," he mused, "if the money was also brought here." Suddenly his eye fell on an irregularly shaped, dark, reddish brown spot on the table top. He looked at it intently. "It looks like blood," he said, astonishment in his voice.

Vledder came closer.

"Where?"

"Here, on the table. They must have been drops of blood. It looks like coagulated blood, you can see the edges of the drops where they were wiped out later."

Momentarily DeKok seemed at a loss. Then he walked with long steps to the beds in the corner. One by one he turned back the covers. The sheets and the pillow of one of the beds were covered with large blood stains.

"Good grief," he exclaimed, "one of the guys is wounded. Constable Bever must have hit somebody, after all."

For a while both stared at the blood stains in the bed.

"I do hope," sighed DeKok, "That the guy had the courage to go see a doctor with that wound . . ."

He did not finish the sentence.

Vledder looked a question at him.

"Do you really think it's serious?"

DeKok nodded slowly.

"Yes, at first glance it seems that he lost a lot of blood. Without medical attention ... " He stopped suddenly. His sharp ears had heard a new sound.

Quickly he indicated to Vledder to position himself next to the door. Softly, without a sound, he went to the switch and turned off the light.

The soft noise of footsteps could be heard from the warehouse space.

12

In darkness, backs against the wall, the two Inspectors listened to the footsteps for seconds that seemed to stretch into hours. The footsteps came closer. Undeniably, inevitably. But the sound became less distinct. It was if the steps had become more cautious, more hesitating, as if sensing an unknown danger. They stopped on the other side of the door.

Vledder, who kept his fingers into light contact with the door, felt a slight pressure. Softly the door was pushed open ... farther, a little farther, until it opened all the way. With tensed muscles, like a runner at the starting block, Vledder waited for a sign from DeKok.

Suddenly the light was switched on. Vledder jumped. With all the power and strength of his athletic body he threw himself on the intruding figure. For a split second the shape was clearly delineated against the bare bulb hanging from the ceiling. It was the silhouette of a woman in a fur coat.

* * *

In the large detective room, against the grim decor of yellowed folders, dusty binders and much abused furniture, the gray sleuth executed a polite bow with old-world formality.

"As I told you," he said with a winning smile, "my name is DeKok, with . . . eh, kay-oh-kay. Please do not consider this conversation as a formal arrest. It's anything *but* an arrest. But I thought it better to talk here, rather than in the warehouse. I'd just like to talk to you for a while." He gestured with a broad grin. "Not an unnatural desire, after all, don't you agree? Your . . . eh, your unexpected visit to Farmer's Alley would naturally arouse our curiosity."

She did not answer. She stared at the two Inspectors. There was a melancholy look in her bright, green eyes, not unlike that of a helpless child looking for protection.

Slowly she unbuttoned her coat and pushed it off her shoulders. It was a studied gesture that indicated refinement and a lot of experience. Only now did it become clear how truly beautiful she was. The dark fur coat had veiled her figure, hid her supple shape.

DeKok looked at her transfixed. She was, he concluded, a ripe, mild beauty, an intoxicating, magical expression of subtle enticement.

"I . . . I hope," he stammered, "that . . . that my colleague's impulsive attack didn't, eh . . . damage you in any way?" He almost blushed because he could not at once find the right words. "After all," he continued, hesitantly, "we . . . couldn't have known that . . . eh, that . . ."

She smiled faintly.

"That it would be me," she completed.

She had a rich, deep voice that vibrated melodically.

DeKok swallowed.

"Exactly, that's how it was. We had not expected such a charming visitor. We were prepared for somewhat 'heavier' visitors."

Another smile briefly shaped her lips.

"Please be assured that the surprise was mutual," she said in a friendly tone of voice. "The last thing I expected to find in that old warehouse was the police. I was looking for my husband."

DeKok's eyebrows seemed poised to ripple, but they merely vibrated slightly. Almost disappointed, Vledder released a small sigh.

"Your husband?" asked DeKok.

She nodded.

"I hoped to find him there. You see, last night he didn't come home at the usual time. I thought it rather strange, I'm not used to that. He's a very precise man, punctual and considerate in all things. If he expected to be late, he would always call. But he did not call last night and after a while I became worried. I had the feeling something had happened. I even searched his desk and checked his pocket calendar and ..."

She stopped abruptly. She looked at the old Inspector with wide-eyed fear.

"Has something happened to my husband," she asked apprehensively. "I mean, your presence in that old warehouse could, ... eh, did it have anything to do with my husband?"

She looked genuinely concerned.

DeKok smiled.

"How can I tell you, Ma'am. I don't even know who you are."

She blushed.

"I'm sorry," she said apologetically. "You didn't ask, but I should have introduced myself. It was very rude of me, but you understand, the shock. Frankly, the whole business has me a bit confused."

DeKok nodded.

"I understand. But perhaps you would be so good as to correct the oversight?"

She smiled coyly.

"I'm Mrs. Thornbush."

There was a sudden silence. It seemed as if the raucous noises from the street had suddenly been stilled by a giant, hidden master switch. The only sound in the detective room was the clattering of the pen that had fallen from Vledder's hand.

DeKok swallowed his surprise.

"Mrs. . . . eh, Mrs. Thornbush?"

"Yes."

DeKok swallowed again.

"Your husband is a VP and Corporate Secretary for Bent & Goossens, for B&G?"

She nodded cheerfully.

"You know him?"

DeKok sighed deeply.

"I . . . eh, I met him once," he said after a slight hesitation. "That was this morning, at the offices of B&G at the Emperor's Canal. Your husband was most cooperative. You see, my colleague and I have been assigned to investigate the hold-up of the armored truck."

Her face became serious.

"Oh, yes, the hold-up. My husband told me about it. It was rather a bold move, I seem to remember. In the center of the city and in broad daylight. It must be difficult for you to find the perpetrators." She lifted her head toward him, admiration in her open, green eyes. "I've often wondered how the police solve all those crimes. I think it's pretty ingenious."

DeKok rubbed his chin and gave her a broad grin. Meanwhile his sharp eyes looked intently at her face, searched for signs of insincerity. He could not detect any. Mrs. Thornbush was calm and at ease, relaxed. A very nice, attractive and above all, naive lady. His professional suspicion could not reach any other conclusion.

"So, you were looking for your husband?"

"Yes."

"And you found the Farmer's Alley address in his note book, his pocket agenda?"

She made a comical gesture.

"My husband will be furious. Believe me, I know him. When he hears what I've done, there will be the devil to pay. He just doesn't like for me to go through his desk. We have argued about that before."

DeKok coughed.

"No doubt, there were more addresses in the book. What made you decide to go to Farmer's Alley?"

She smiled.

"The date ... the address was listed under today's date."

"Was there any other information? A name, or a time?"

She shrugged her shoulders.

"No, just *warehouse, Farmer's Alley, Amsterdam*," she sighed. "That was all."

"Did you notice ... I mean, did the address appear more than once in the appointment book?"

She grimaced.

"I didn't look any further. I immediately went on my way."

"How were you able to find Farmer's Alley. Did you know where it was?"

She shook her head.

"No, I was born and raised in Amsterdam, but I'd never heard of it. I took a cab at the station." She grinned while she wrinkled her nose. "The driver asked me several times to repeat the address. Apparently he thought it strange that I would want to go there."

DeKok nodded understanding.

"How did you get to the station?"

"Well, I arrived by train from Haarlem. That's where I live."

"Do you live close to a Mr. Bergen, another VP at B&G?"

Her eyes flashed momentarily.

"Bergen lives to the south of Haarlem, we live more to the north of the city."

DeKok scratched the back of his neck.

"But you were sure your husband was no longer in the office? He could have worked late, or perhaps there was a meeting?"

"I called the office," she answered softly. "I reached the security guard. He told me that my husband had left at the usual time, at about the same time as the others."

"Perhaps he stopped over with business relations, or friends . . . family perhaps?"

She shook her head.

"We have few contacts with others. We live rather a retiring life."

DeKok sighed.

"So, you haven't the faintest idea about the where-abouts of your husband?"

She moved slightly in the chair.

"No," she answered in a sudden, vehement tone of voice. "What do you think? Otherwise I certainly wouldn't have dragged myself all the way to Farmer's Alley. Believe me, I had to overcome a great deal of fear, of apprehension, before I dared enter that dark warehouse."

DeKok nodded at her in a friendly way.

"You're a courageous woman," he said, admiration in his voice. "Also," he continued, "you apparently care a great deal about your husband."

She looked at him with suspicion.

"Yes," she said, tentatively, "yes," firmer this time, "yes, I do."

The acting watch-commander, Scholten, entered the room at that point. He carried a note in his hand.

"Dammit, DeKok," he growled, "I've looked for you everywhere. I even had them check as far as Maltese Cross Alley. Why can we never reach you on the radio? Greanheather told me just now that you were back."

DeKok looked at him with amazement.

"But what can the matter be?"

"That woman called again."

"When?"

"About an hour ago, you had just left."

"Well?"

Scholten looked hesitantly at the woman in the chair in front of DeKok's desk. He pondered how explicit he could be in her presence.

"She gave me a message for you. I wrote it down."

DeKok took the note from him and read:

Thornbush has two airline tickets for Houston, USA.

Thoughtfully he pulled on his lower lip and then let it plop back. He did that several times. It was a most annoying sound.

"You're certain it was the same woman?" he asked finally.

"Yes, undoubtedly."

"You couldn't be mistaken?"

"It was the same voice. It was recorded, you know." Scholten gave the explanation almost automatically, knowing that DeKok would disdain such esoteric developments as the automatic recording of all incoming calls.

"Did she identify herself?" asked DeKok, sublimely indifferent to the subconscious by-play.

"I tried, of course, but she refused to tell her name."

DeKok crushed the piece of paper in a ball and threw it in the nearest waste basket. He looked up at the acting watch-commander and asked:

"Did she say anything else? I mean, besides what was in the note?"

Scholten shook his head.

"She said no other explanation was needed. You would know exactly what the message meant."

DeKok pressed his lips together into a tight line.

"Thank you," he said.

Scholten turned around and left the room without another word. He was acting watch-commander but for some reason DeKok nevertheless always intimidated him. Strange really, the man would never be promoted past his present rank. He was too much of a maverick for that. But his age and above all, his thorough understanding of police work, seemed to force respect from all his colleagues, high or low.

Mrs. Thornbush leaned forward and placed a hand lightly on DeKok's forearm.

"News about my husband?" she asked fearfully.

The gray sleuth looked at her for a long moment and then he slowly shook his head.

"No," he lied blandly, "not about your husband. But we must ask you to excuse us. The message makes it necessary that we continue with an ongoing investigation." He gave her a winning smile, trying to soothe the pomposity in his voice. "I think it best," he added with a fatherly firmness, "that you go back to Haarlem. Perhaps your husband has come home in the meantime and you'll find you've been worrying about nothing at all, at all."

"He isn't home," she replied seriously.

"What?"

"He isn't home," she repeated insistently.

DeKok gave her a searching look. There had been a strange tone in her voice. It gave him a queazy feeling. As if she had spoken with an inner conviction, based on immutable facts.

"Why not?"

She shrugged her shoulders and at the same time pulled up the fur coat and pulled it tighter around her body. She shivered visibly.

"I'm afraid, Inspector," she said hoarsely, almost in a whisper, "I'm afraid that something has happened to my husband. Something serious, I mean." She tapped her ample chest with the tips of her fingers. "Deep inside me I have the terrible feeling that I will never again see my husband alive." She made a sad gesture. A single tear rolled down her cheek and dripped on her fur coat.

"I know it's silly," she sobbed. "I try to fight it, but it doesn't work . . . it doesn't work. I can't get rid of that terrible feeling."

* * *

Inspector Vledder whipped the police VW along the road to Schiphol Airport. He held the steering wheel in a firm grip and there was a determined look on his face.

131

"I hope we make it," he said, irritation in his voice. "Once that plane leaves the ground we can't do anything about it." He risked a glance at his older colleague. "Didn't I see you on the phone? Why didn't you at the same time alert the State Police and Airport Security? You could have asked them to arrest Thornbush at the airport. They would have been happy to comply."

DeKok smiled.

"Certainly. But why should I ask them to arrest Thornbush?"

Vledder made an unexpected movement, almost causing the small car to leave the road.

"Why?" he asked in amazement. "You ask WHY? But isn't it crystal clear that he's the man behind the hold-up? Everything points to it. Just think. He was almost certainly the man who accepted Geffel's phone call. You tried a similar call yourself. He was also the man who kept in contact with the robbers. Just think about the note in his appointment book about Farmer's Alley." He paused, his attention on the road. Then he snorted and added: "And he's the man who's on the verge of absconding with the loot."

DeKok raised a restraining hand.

"Just a moment, my friend," he laughed. "You're going too fast. The loot . . . the loot hasn't left the country and isn't going to leave the country. That's one of the advantages of living in a small country like ours. There are precious few places to hide and there are none where you can hide for long. Besides, I asked Customs at Schiphol to thoroughly search Thornbush *and* his luggage. Every cubic centimeter of his luggage will be searched."

Vledder shrugged his shoulders.

"But I still think it would have been simpler just to arrest him at the airport. Then we would have had it all: perpetrator and loot."

DeKok ignored the remark.

"Also," he continued as if Vledder had not said a word, "I made a deal."

"A deal?"

DeKok nodded, self-satisfied.

"Yes, I made a deal with the Customs people. If they were to find any large quantities of money, jewels, gold, or any other valuables in the luggage, they would alert the State Police to arrest Thornbush. Not before."

He looked aside at Vledder and grimaced.

"We don't want a VP without loot. If, after his arrest, he were to refuse to tell us about it, about the three million—and he would be crazy if he told us—we would still be as far from the solution as before. You understand?" He paused, glanced at the road, shrugged and continued. "Without the loot our case rests on a notation in a pocket calendar book. Four words: warehouse, Farmer's Alley, Amsterdam. A very narrow basis for a conviction." He shook his head. "No, Dick, if the Customs people don't find anything, we're better off letting our Secretary go, in the hope that he will eventually lead us to the money. Without the money he isn't about to stay in Houston."

They drove on in silence after that. Suddenly Vledder slowed down. With open mouth he looked at DeKok.

"B-but . . . ," he stuttered, "b-but if it's all taken care of, then why are we racing to the airport?"

DeKok grinned broadly.

"Thornbush has *two* tickets. I'm dying to know who's flying on the second ticket."

133

13

Mr. Westerhoff, Assistant Bureau Chief of Customs at Schiphol Airport pointed at the lights of a 747 as it rose into the air near the end of a runway.

"There she goes," he said with a wide grin, "Destination: Houston in the good old U. S. of A."

DeKok stared after the lights for a long time until they melded into the distance. Then he turned slowly toward the Customs man.

"And?"

"Nothing."

"What nothing?"

"He didn't show up. Everybody had been instructed, everybody was alert. All for nothing. He was a no-show."

DeKok's eyebrows rippled briefly. Westerhoff suddenly looked at him intently, as if he could not believe his own eyes.

"So, the plane left without him?" asked DeKok.

The Assistant Bureau Chief shook his head, as if clearing his vision and raised his hands in a helpless gesture.

"I presume so. There was certainly nobody aboard that looked like the description we received of Thornbush."

"Was he listed as a passenger?"

"Oh, yes. We checked that first. Thornbush was on the passenger's manifest."

"Alone?"

"What do you mean?"

DeKok sighed, a bit impatiently.

"According to our information, he had two tickets. Did he travel alone? Was he listed singly on the manifest? I wonder in what name the second ticket was issued."

Westerhoff looked at him with surprise.

"His wife, of course," he responded.

DeKok's mouth fell open.

"Wife?"

"Yes, yes, I thought you knew. They were listed as Mr. and Mrs. Thornbush."

* * *

At a very sedate pace they drove back to Amsterdam. DeKok was sprawled comfortably in the passenger seat next to Vledder. The greenish light from the communication gear gave his friendly face the contradictory expression of a devil that had been banished from Hell because of its innate goodness. He grinned softly to himself. Vledder looked aside.

"Wife," remarked DeKok mockingly. "I don't think that KLM asks for marriage certificates."

Vledder looked at him defiantly.

"And you do?"

DeKok looked at him.

"What *do* you mean?"

It was Vledder's turn to grin.

"Do you ask for marriage certificates? I don't seem to recall that you asked for any identification from the woman

136

we surprised in the Farmer's Alley. You certainly didn't ask for a marriage certificate."

DeKok shook his head.

"No, I didn't. But I can tell you that she was born about thirty-five years ago under the name of Judith Klarenbeek in the Old Wilhelmina Hospital in Amsterdam. Before she married Thornbush she was a dancer of some renown."

"And how did you find all that out?"

"I had it checked out. By the way, nothing detrimental or disreputable is known about the couple. No police records, anyway."

Vledder stared pensively at the road.

"In any case she wasn't the woman that was listed as Mrs. Thornbush on the passenger's manifest."

DeKok smiled.

"A logical conclusion. The real Mrs. Thornbush wouldn't have been looking for her husband in Farmer's Alley if she had made a date to meet him at Schiphol." He paused for a moment. "Although . . ."

"Although, what?"

"Perhaps the trip to Houston was a secret that Mrs. Thornbush wasn't about to reveal to us."

Vledder gave him a penetrating look.

"In other words, the Mrs. Thornbush on the manifest was the real Mrs. Thornbush, but Mr. Thornbush, for whatever reason, was prevented from meeting her."

DeKok nodded slowly.

"It could be that way," he reflected. "In any case it's a possibility we shouldn't overlook. Yet, at the same time, it's probably better to give the wife on the manifest no name at this time. Let's just call her 'Second Ticket' for the time being. It prevents surprises. After all, feisty men like Thornbush often have a weakness for amorous adventures."

Vledder laughed.

For a while they drove on in companionable silence. Vledder kept his eyes on the road. His youthful face was serious. There was a deep crease in his forehead. He was thinking.

"You know," he said suddenly, "we've got three of them."

DeKok looked at him with expectation.

"Three what?"

"Women with whom Thornbush is involved, or women who are involved with Thornbush. In any case, women who know him well. It certainly seems to confirm your suspicion of Thornbush as some sort of Lothario. What did you call him? . . . feisty?"

"Go on," growled DeKok.

Vledder grinned.

"Three women. Count them. The real wife, 'Second Ticket' wife and the woman who called."

DeKok's eyebrows vibrated slightly, then rippled definitely.

"You mean the woman who tipped us about the ticket?"

Vledder nodded.

"Exactly. And that's the most important woman for us. Just think. First of all, she knew that Thornbush was planning to leave the country and second . . . that you were interested in that fact. Especially the last is interesting. It means, I think, that she either knows, or suspects, the relationship between the hold-up and . . . Thornbush."

DeKok pressed his heavy body into a more upright position and looked at his former pupil with pride.

"Excellent," he said with admiration in his voice, "really excellent. I couldn't have done better myself. Crystal clear reasoning. That third woman is indeed the most important for our investigation."

Vledder blushed under the onslaught of that much praise.

"It's just too bad," he said with a regretful tone of voice, "that we don't know who she is. Perhaps she could tell us who 'Second Ticket' was."

"And," supplied DeKok, "maybe she can tell us why Thornbush did not go on the trip after all, why it was cancelled because of lack of interest."

They had reached the city. The streets were deserted at this late hour. No buses, no streetcars. An occasional milk-float could be heard rattling along the canals.

DeKok rubbed his eyes with the back of his hand.

"Take me home," he yawned. "I want to get some sleep. Tomorrow is another day."

Vledder guided the car to DeKok's house.

"Any other plans?" he asked casually.

DeKok nodded slowly.

"As soon as you wake up, I want you to go back to Haarlem. You ask Mrs. Thornbush if her husband has shown up in the meantime. Be sincere, show interest. Try to take a look around."

"And?"

"What?"

"If he has shown up?"

DeKok shrugged his shoulders in a careless gesture.

"Then you show her your pearly whites in a most winning smile and in your most ingratiating tone of voice you declare that it's usual for beautiful women to worry about their husbands. And if Mr. Vice President *hasn't* shown up, you promise most sincerely that we'll move heaven and earth to find him."

Vledder nodded his understanding.

"And what about you?"

DeKok rubbed his hands together as if in anticipated pleasure. He grinned.

"I'm going to see my good friend Little Lowee. I'm curious about the price of whiskey, these days."

* * *

With a friendly grin on his large, somewhat melancholy face, DeKok strolled along the Rear Fort Canal. A few hours of sleep had banished the tiredness from his bones and he was again fully prepared to face a world of crime. Cheerfully he greeted a number of "good" guys and "bad" girls and brought his old friend Handy Henkie close to a heart-attack when he suddenly lowered his heavy hand on the shoulder of the ex-burglar. Henkie's left leg was in a cast and he supported himself with a crutch.

He seemed to shrink when he felt DeKok's hand and turned with some difficulty. His face was pale and there was a hunted look in his eyes. He breathed a sigh of relief when he discerned the old sleuth.

"Dammit, DeKok," he said, shaking his head, "you shouldn't of done that. Geez, you shoulda known I've given it all up. But yet ... you see, iffen I feel a hand on me shoulder, I gets the willies."

DeKok smiled.

"Not working?"

Henkie gestured toward his left leg.

"Some fool done dropped a hunk of iron on me foot."

"You're sure?" asked DeKok with suspicion in his voice but with a broad grin on his face. "You're sure it was a *work* related accident?"

Henkie looked at him without guile.

"Of course it were! You can see for yourself. I've got Workman's Compensation and everything. Wadda difference from the old days. Then, iffen something happened to me, I'd have to hole up and too afraid to see a doctor. Now, the doctor says its gonna be a few more weeks."

DeKok pulled a serious face.

"Still," he said with a sympathetic voice, "it isn't something you would wish on anybody. Anyway," he said, changing the tone and the direction of the conversation, "at least you'll have time to have a drink with me. My treat."

Henkie grinned.

"Alla time in the world," he declared.

Next to DeKok he hobbled along to the well-known underworld bar of Little Lowee.

They pushed the heavy curtains aside and entered the bar. This early in the morning they were the only visitors. Lowee was behind the bar and polished glasses. He greeted them jovially. DeKok and Handy Henkie walked toward the back of the dimly lit room and sat down at one of the small tables. Henkie pulled up an extra chair and placed his injured leg on it.

"I've gotta rest it," he explained.

DeKok nodded his understanding.

Little Lowee shuffled closer. He carried a tray with two bottles and three glasses.

"Come on and join us," invited DeKok. "My treat."

Lowee grinned.

"How come? Is it your birthday?"

DeKok shook his head.

"No, that's a few more months in the offing. But I have just about solved the case of the hold-up." He made a nonchalant gesture. "And that's worth celebrating, don't you agree?"

Henkie snorted.

"It all depends how you looks at it," he said mockingly. "Iffen you ask me, it ain't exactly a reason to get all happy about."

DeKok carefully watched Lowee's reactions. He noticed a tic near the right eye of the small barkeeper.

"I ain't seen nothing about it in the papers," he remarked while he poured generously.

DeKok heard a vague suspicion in the tone of voice.

"Well," he said expansively, "I figure the Commissaris probably doesn't want the press to know yet. He'll probably wait until after I've arrested the perpetrators. Otherwise they might take off prematurely, you know. We don't want to give them any warning, after all. No, no, we want to prevent that at all cost. We aim for a speedy arrest." He paused for effect. "I just hope it won't take much longer. We could be too late."

Handy Henkie looked at him with astonishment.

"Too late?"

DeKok nodded. His face was serious.

"One of the boys was wounded during the hold-up. A constable shot him in the back as they were fleeing the scene of the crime. We know the man has lost a considerable amount of blood. If the bullet wound isn't treated quickly and correctly, it could very well be fatal."

"You means he'll konk off?"

DeKok shook his head in commiseration.

"It's extremely dangerous not to treat a gunshot wound."

Handy Henkie shook his head in desperation.

"But why doesn't that stupid bastard give himself up? I means, how much is he likely gonna get? Two years? Give him a good chance to get cured all the way."

DeKok turned the glass in his hands. Pensively he stared into the distance.

"Murder . . . you get a little more than two years for murder."

Lowee sat up abruptly. His mousey face was red and his adam's apple bobbed up and down.

"Those boys," he exclaimed with passion, "ain't got nothin' to do with Pete's killing."

DeKok looked at him in well feigned surprise.

"Well," he said calmly, "that's an extremely positive statement." He leaned back in his chair and stared evenly at Lowee. "If you don't mind my asking, I would be very interested to know how you gained that particular insight?"

The small barkeeper swallowed. A blue vein throbbed in his neck. A distinct tic developed along his high cheekbones.

"Well . . . I, I just thought . . ."

DeKok rubbed the bridge of his nose with a little finger.

"I seem to remember," he said slowly, with emphasis, "that you thought the opposite during our last conference." He curled his lips up and displayed a frightening, false grin. "Or," he added, "did you change your opinion because they bought their whiskey from you?"

14

Little Lowee was pale. Sweat beaded his forehead and his hair seemed to be plastered to his head.

"Whiskey? I don't know nothing about no whiskey."

DeKok pushed his chair back a bit.

"Come, come, Lowee. You know very well what I'm talking about." He made a grand gesture. "Whiskey in an old, abandoned warehouse in Farmer's Alley."

The barkeeper swallowed.

"I don't know," he repeated stubbornly, "wadda you talking about."

DeKok rubbed his face with a flat hand. From between his spread fingers he looked searchingly at Lowee.

"Lowee," he said with just a hint of impatience, "please reflect ... how long have I been visiting your ... eh, your establishment? Fifteen years? Twenty years? Not much longer and I'll be celebrating my Silver Anniversary here." He grinned mockingly. "Now do you understand? I am not mistaken. I recognize a bottle from your bar from a mile away."

Handy Henkie looked from DeKok to Lowee and back again. Then he picked up his glass and emptied it in one swallow.

"I thinks," he sighed, "I better hit the road." With a painful grimace he lifted his left leg from the extra chair. "You guys is getting too pally for me."

DeKok waved goodbye to him but held Lowee in his uninterrupted gaze.

"See you around," he said, "and I hope your leg gets better soon."

Henkie hobbled away.

"Thanks," he tossed over his shoulder, "you knows where to find me."

Then he disappeared between the leather-bordered curtains. A little later they heard the door slam behind him.

DeKok stood up.

"Where can I find the guys?"

Lowee shook his head.

"I don't know," his voice was curt.

DeKok sighed.

"One of the boys is in bad shape," he exclaimed despondently. "Don't you understand? You just can't sit there and let that guy bleed to death. It just isn't worth it."

Lowee pressed his lips together.

"I cain't tell you a thing."

DeKok bit his lower lip.

"Then I will make you a promise," he said threateningly. "If that boy dies of his wounds . . . if he dies, I'll hold *you* responsible. Now, for the last time: where are they?"

Little Lowee raised his arms in a gesture of despair and confusion.

"I don't know. I don't know, I tole you. They don't tell me everything!"

Slowly DeKok shook his head.

"I told you before, Lowee," he said calmly. "You're a bad liar." He took the slender barkeeper by the shoulder and gently pushed him forward. "Just close the place and get your black suit out of the mothballs. We're going to a funeral."

"Funeral?"

DeKok nodded.

"Yes, Pete Geffel's funeral."

Lowee looked at him. There was fear in his eyes.

"I . . . eh, I cain't," he stammered. "I-I I've gotta . . ."

DeKok waved his protest away.

"Just put a sign up for your whiskey clients," he said cynically, "Say: *Closed because of death* and hang it on the door."

* * *

A watery winter sun pinked through the high, narrow windows of the Chapel, reflected off the pulpit and shined playfully on the bald skull of the minister who spoke in pregnant tones of love, death and resurrection. As is common in Holland, the Chapel was non-denominational and actually stood on the grounds of the cemetery. Convenient, thought DeKok sardonically, and so wise of our early ancestors. It certainly kept the costs down.

DeKok stood toward the rear, his back against the oak panelling and rocked softly to the cadence of the minister's words. Little Lowee stood next to him, estranged, ill at ease, in a subdued, black suit.

The gray cop let his gaze wander through the Chapel.

Mother Geffel was seated close to the flower-bedecked coffin. Her head was bent and she plucked nervously at a minuscule handkerchief in her lap. Next to her, sitting straight and unmoving, was Flossie. He kept his gaze on her for a long time. Outwardly she seemed unmoved, distant. But there was a determined set to her mouth.

DeKok feared for the girl. He was afraid of her irreconcilable persistence. In her present state of mind he judged her capable of anything. He wondered what he could do to protect her from herself, but could not find a reasonable solution. Again he looked at her. The black scarf on her head accentuated the wax-like paleness of her fine face.

After the minister, Gus Shenk climbed the pulpit for the eulogy. As could be expected, old man Shenk was straightforward and to the point. He stated that Pete, despite his many missteps, had not deserved to die as he did. It was not fair, according to Gus and despite all talk about "loving thy neighbor', so eloquently described by the minister, he, Gus, hoped that the killer would soon be caught and would not escape his just punishment. And anyone, he announced loudly, who helped hide the murderers from the police, who aided and abetted the scum that had killed Pete Geffel was an accomplice and just as guilty of the murder. He went on to describe Pete as an ordinary boy of the people, a boy with a good heart, who, no matter what anybody said, had always been good for his mother.

A murmur of agreement went through the chapel after those words and Mother Geffel sobbed audibly. DeKok glanced at Little Lowee. The small barkeeper's lower lip trembled and his adam's apple bobbed up and down. Apparently he had difficulty controlling himself. And Shenk acted as if every word was aimed directly at him, at Little Lowee from the disreputable bar in the Barn Alley.

DeKok smiled to himself. As soon as he had heard that Gus Shenk would deliver the eulogy, he had made sure that Lowee would attend the funeral. After all, DeKok knew

"Uncle Gus" and he was hopeful that his speech might just touch a weak string in Lowee's conscience. Perhaps enough to get him to talk about what he knew. And DeKok was convinced that Lowee had a lot to tell.

After the heart-rending speech of the old cop, organ music filled the Chapel. The doors opened and the professional pallbearers lifted the coffin from the stand. Slowly, the visitors followed the coffin to the cemetery grounds.

DeKok held Little Lowee by the arm as they followed at the rear of the procession. At the end of the procession he could gain a good overview of all those present. He had been unable to find any "strange" faces among the spectators in the Chapel. He nudged Lowee.

"If you see one of the guys I'm looking for," he whispered, "I trust you to let me know."

The barkeeper nodded mechanically. For the moment he had no resistance left. The gathering and the echoes of Shenk's eloquence had taken the fight out of him.

DeKok wondered why Lowee was protecting the crooks. There was no denying the fact that the whiskey bottle he had found in the warehouse originated in Lowee's bar. There was no question about it. The label was marked with Lowee's private identification. It was ironic, but it had been DeKok's idea originally. When several years ago Lowee had systematically been robbed by a cleaning lady who absconded with several bottles a day, it had been difficult to find evidence. DeKok had advised the barkeeper to mark his bottles in a certain way. It had become a habit. Again he nudged the barkeeper.

"Well?"

Lowee seemed to recover from a half dazed state.

"The boys ain't here," he retorted sharply. He paused. "And iffen they *was* here, I wouldn't tell ye."

DeKok cocked his head at him.

"So, you *know* who they are."

"Yes."

"And you hid them from me," said DeKok bitterly. "You hid them in that old warehouse."

Lowee shook his head.

"I gave 'em food and something to drink. No more."

DeKok nodded slowly.

"How did you find out they were on Farmer's Alley?"

"Somebody tipped me."

"And where are they now?"

Lowee turned abruptly toward the cop.

"Are we gonna play those games all over again?" His tone was belligerent. "They's gone. They couldn't stay any longer because of the boy. He needed a doc."

"Go on."

Lowee sighed.

"He's being took care of."

"Medical care?"

"That too."

"Why wait so long?"

"Wadda you mean?"

DeKok gave him a hard, long look.

"That boy has for several days been kept on a bunch of rags in the Alley, without anybody taking care of him. Why didn't they get a doctor at once?"

Lowee stared in front of him, avoiding DeKok's eyes.

"Doctors that don't ask questions, cost bread."

DeKok grinned.

"So what? They certainly had plenty."

Lowee did not answer.

DeKok was beginning to get angry. The rigid attitude of the small barkeeper was getting on his nerves. He pressed his lips together, took a deep breath and said:

"After all, there was plenty of money." He hissed the words.

Little Lowee looked pale.

"I," he answered softly, "I paid for the doc."

"You?"

Lowee started to walk faster. He closed up to the end of the procession.

DeKok knew he had to wait for a better opportunity. Perhaps later, in the bar. He fervently hoped that Lowee would come forth on his own account. He had, after all, a weakness for the slender barkeeper and he did not feel like spoiling their friendship of years with an arrest. He shifted his attention back to the procession that slowly moved along the gravel paths of the cemetery. In the forefront, above their heads, the coffin bobbed on the shoulders of the pallbearers. They stopped next to the open grave. The coffin was lifted from the shoulders with routine, much practiced movements and placed on the grave lift. The mourners formed a rough circle around the hole in the ground. DeKok was on the alert. He looked sharply at the faces around him. He always made it a point to attend the funerals of murder victims. He knew so well that there were a number of killers who could not resist attending the funerals of their victims.

Suddenly he saw a face in the circle opposite him. Almost at the rear of the crowd he discovered a man with sharp features in a deeply creased face. It gave DeKok a sudden shock. He had first met the man a short time ago, just a few days. The face seemed to have aged years since the last time he saw it. Their glances crossed each other. Just for a moment. For a short moment in time they looked deep into each other's eyes. Then the man ducked.

Old Gus Shenk stepped forward and expressed thanks on behalf of the family of the deceased. DeKok pulled his head into the collar of his coat and circled around the rear of the crowd to the place where he had seen the man. But the man was gone when he arrived on the spot. With quick steps DeKok followed the gravel paths to the exit. He hoped to be able to overtake the man before he left the cemetery. Numerous questions burned on his tongue. But when he turned the corner of the Chapel, he saw the black Bentley just clear the gate.

DeKok slowed down. He panted for breath. He was not used to exerting himself this way. Pensively he looked after the car. Bent must have run to make it so quickly to his car. Why? Why was he in such a hurry to leave? It seemed more like a flight. After all, it was a free country. He was certainly allowed to attend Pete Geffel's funeral. DeKok decided to call on Bent again, very soon.

* * *

Vledder looked reproachfully at DeKok.

"You could have told me ahead of time that you were going to the funeral."

"Why?"

Vledder made an impatient gesture.

"If I had known, I would have come straight to the cemetery from Haarlem. Now I've wasted two hours waiting for you."

DeKok's eyebrows vibrated briefly and then stilled.

"Wasted time?" he asked, surprised. "But surely you could have used those two hours productively."

152

A slight suspicion seemed to glimmer in Vledder's eyes.

"What could I have done?" he asked, unsure of himself.

"Think," was the laconic reply. "You could have spent your time thinking. For instance: who killed Peter Geffel, aka *Cunning Pete* and why? Who actually executed the hold-up? Did they really steal three million? If so, where is the money? If not, who committed fraud? As you see, there was no need to 'waste' two hours. There are plenty of problems."

Vledder nodded willingly.

"You're right," he said. His face and his voice were serious. "There are indeed plenty of problems. Too many, if you ask me. There seems to be little progress. Things don't compute. We've been at it for four days already and we're almost as far as we were in the beginning. It's disheartening."

DeKok raised a hand in protest.

"I don't agree with you there. We just haven't yet figured out how the various pieces fit together. That's about it. It still looks very much like a jig-saw puzzle and so far we only have a few pieces in place. But I'm confident that we'll solve the mystery before long. We're a lot closer to the guys that committed the robbery, for instance."

Vledder looked at him with bewilderment.

"Why do you say that? We know where they *used* to hang out, at Farmer's Alley. But that's all."

DeKok smiled.

"This morning, more or less under duress, Little Lowee told me that he knew them."

"But that's great."

"Perhaps. But he wasn't about to reveal any names. He admitted that he knew about the warehouse and he admitted that he supplied them with food and drink. The whiskey bottle, for instance, came from his bar."

"And what else?"

"What do you mean . . . what else?"

Vledder made a peevish gesture.

"Surely you tried to get him to talk?"

DeKok sighed.

"Of course I tried, Dick. I tried just about everything to get him to talk. I even forced him to come to Pete's funeral in the hope of weakening him. Lowee is a pretty sentimental guy, you know. But nothing worked."

"So, now what?"

DeKok shrugged his shoulders.

"I don't know," he answered hesitantly. "There's something strange about Lowee's attitude. You see, a robbery is a robbery. But murder is a different kettle of fish altogether." He paused, gathered his thoughts. "Especially in Amsterdam. Among the regular crowd of criminals, murder is taken very seriously, indeed. I don't mean to include the drug trade, you know. No, among the robbers, the burglars, the petty thieves, in short, among the common criminals murder is almost unheard of. And when one of their own is killed, the whole underworld is against them. Lowee must really feel very strongly that the robbers had nothing to do with Pete's killing."

"How does that follow?"

"Well, I don't think that Lowee would have taken care of them, otherwise, or that he would have kept it a secret from me if he had even the slightest doubt about their innocence. Lowee is an old-fashioned crook, so to speak."

Vledder laughed scornfully.

"Three million is a lot of money."

DeKok's eyebrows rippled in earnest this time.

"What do you mean by that remark?"

Vledder shrugged his shoulder.

"Nothing," he said reluctantly, unable to tear his gaze away from DeKok's forehead. "Nothing. I just mean to say ... that ... a lot of people have done worse for a lot less money."

DeKok looked intently at his protegee.

"You're rather cynical, all of a sudden."

Vledder sighed elaborately.

"Ach," he said, obviously irritated. It was not quite certain with what, or with whom he was irritated. "You're probably right. Lowee is indeed an 'honest' crook. After all, you know him a lot better than me. But the whole case bothers me, that's all. I just can't see an end to it. It's all so vague, so, so ... circumstantial. If the perpetrators of the robbery aren't guilty of Pete's death, who is?"

DeKok did not answer. He stood up from his chair and started to pace up and down the detective room. Every once in a while he would look at Vledder who remained seated with a rebellious look on his face. The younger man stared obstinately into the distance. DeKok wondered if, perhaps, he had not given him enough to do, or maybe he had given him the less important role. Possibly he had done his younger colleague an injustice, not shared enough with him.

He stopped in front of Vledder.

"You were in Haarlem. Has Thornbush surfaced yet?"

Vledder shook his head.

"No, he's now been missing since last night and Mrs. Thornbush is getting more and more worried. She *looked* worried. Apparently she was awake all night. Even before I showed up, she had already called his office three times. But Thornbush hasn't appeared there, either."

DeKok nodded slowly.

"Then what did you do?"

"I took as accurate a description from Mrs. Thornbush as she could give me. She also gave me a photo. I added the facts we already know. Then I prepared an APB and had it transmitted from Haarlem. I requested location and apprehension."

DeKok nodded approval.

"Nothing much else you could do, under the circumstances." He paused and pulled on his lower lip. There was a pensive look in his eyes. Then he said: "Yet, the mysterious disappearance of Thornbush is a remarkable coincidence. I don't believe in coincidences. We'd do well to keep a close eye on that development." He rubbed the bridge of his nose with a little finger. "I wonder where the man can be?" he added.

The phone rang at that moment. DeKok lifted the receiver.

"I saw you at the cemetery." Despite the whispering tones, DeKok immediately recognized Flossie' voice. "I half expected that you would have a cup of coffee with me after the funeral." She laughed without humor. "As a sort of compensation for the coffee you didn't drink at my place."

"I . . . I ran out of time. As you know, I'm also investigating a murder."

"Any news?"

"No."

"Oh."

For a long time it remained silent on the other end of the line. Then she said:

"Did you know that Thornbush has a long-standing affair with Bent's young wife?"

15

"Hello . . . hello!"

DeKok threw the receiver back on the hook.

"She hung up."

"Who?"

"Flossie. She wanted to know if I had any news and when I answered in the negative, she asked if I knew that Thornbush had an affair with Bent's wife."

Vledder grinned.

"The Secretary and the wife of the President."

DeKok nodded.

"Indeed, an interesting twist on an almost classical situation."

Vledder's eyes lit up.

"Perhaps Mrs. Bent is 'Second Ticket'?"

DeKok pushed his lower lip forward.

"She could also have been the woman who sent us to Schiphol last night. In any case, as long as he doesn't show up, it may be a good idea to keep an eye on the women around our elusive Secretary. One of them probably knows where he is."

Vledder looked at him.

"Do you think that the disappearance of Thornbush means little more than that he's stepping out on his wife?"

Inspector DeKok pulled a serious face and shook his head.

"It's more. It means a lot more than that. The disappearance of Thornbush is important to the case as a whole. I firmly believe that Thornbush really planned to flee the country last night. It would be interesting to know what prevented him."

"Perhaps he picked a different escape route at the last moment."

"Possibly, but then there had to be something that caused him to change his original plans. I wonder what that could have been."

* * *

They remained silent for a long time. DeKok pulled his legs up and placed them on top of the desk and leaned comfortably back in his chair. His forced march on the cemetery was having its effect. Vledder was the first to break the silence.

"But you know what I don't understand? Why would Thornbush run off? We have no proof at all of his complicity, either with the robbery, or with Pete's killing. To flee like that would only make sense if he had the loot."

"And?"

"What ... and?"

"And why shouldn't he be in possession of the loot?"

Vledder looked stupefied.

"You forget about the guys that did the actual hold-up. After all, they didn't do that just for amusement."

"You mean, they wouldn't just hand over the proceeds?"

"Exactly."

"And if there was fraud as well?" asked DeKok thoughtfully.

Vledder creased his forehead, the closest he could come to frowning in DeKok's inimitable manner.

"Aha, you're starting to take our theory serious! You believe there may very well be a difference between the reported amount and the actual amount. Insurance fraud seems more possible to you?"

"Yes."

Vledder shook his head.

"Well, you see, I have problems with that. At least in connection with Thornbush. I just don't think it would be all that easy for him to set something like that up all by himself."

DeKok gestured.

"Even so, he could have possession of the loot. You understand, even with the connivance of one, or more of the other members of management. After all, if it *is* a matter of fraud, the accomplices would hardly start to divvy up the loot at once. Thus it would not be at all unusual if Thornbush had been appointed to take care of the money until the spoils could be divided. No, not unlikely at all, at all."

"Then, why don't we arrest the whole bunch?"

DeKok grinned wickedly.

"For the same reasons as last night. In fact, nothing has really changed."

Vledder looked at him for a long time, deep in thought.

"Do you think . . . ," he began after a while, hesitantly, looking for words. "Do you . . . eh, think that Thornbush on his own, last night . . . I mean, without telling his accomplices . . . that he might have attempted to take off with all the money? And that . . . eh, maybe that became known somehow?"

DeKok nodded slowly.

"Something like that . . . yes."

Vledder swallowed.

"B-but . . . but," he stammered, "in that case, in that case the disappearance of Thornbush means something entirely different. Then . . ." He stopped, confused.

DeKok nodded encouragingly.

"Go on," he said.

The young Inspector swallowed once more.

"In that case Thornbush committed treason, I mean . . . he betrayed his accomplices. You know what that means, DeKok? These are people who are not afraid to kill. We've seen that already with Pete Geffel. If we don't find Thornbush real soon, I don't give a plugged nickel for his chances of survival."

* * *

They found the missing Simca about halfway between Amsterdam and Utrecht near a small village along the banks of a smaller river with the incongruous name of Joy, just past the old windmill that had seen better days. The shiny bumper was pressed hard against a pair of rotting willows with bare branches that poked at the gray sky. At first glance there seemed to be no damage to the exterior of the vehicle, until one noticed the two bullet holes in the trunk.

Sergeant-Major Windt of the State Police leaned against his bicycle close by with a bored look on his face. He looked at the two Inspectors from Amsterdam.

"I think," said the sergeant-major in a gravelly voice, "that the car must have been placed there last night, during the night I mean. Last *evening*, during my last rounds, it wasn't there. I'm sure of that. I couldn't have missed it. I saw it for the first time this afternoon."

"At what time?"

"About two o'clock. I had just come from Town Hall," he waved vaguely in the direction of a church tower in the distance. "Then I started my afternoon rounds." He nodded, pursed his lips and repeated: "Yes, it must have been just after two."

DeKok nodded.

"We're very grateful for your prompt notification," he said formally.

"Yes, well, I saw at once that it was the car you were looking for. The two bullet holes were clear enough."

DeKok smiled.

"Did you search the car?"

The sergeant-major shook his head emphatically.

"No," he growled, "I kept my hands off it. You never know what you might spoil. I looked through the windows, that's all. The keys are still in the ignition. And ... I think I saw blood on the rear seat."

DeKok pushed his old hat forward until it almost obscured his eyes.

"That's possible," he said slowly. "One of our constables shot at the fleeing car. That explains the bullet holes. Possibly he hit one of the occupants." He turned to Vledder. "Alert the fingerprint experts and the photographer. Also order a wrecker." He turned back to the sergeant-major and gave him a winning smile. "I take it that you have no objection if we confiscate the vehicle?"

The broad-shouldered State cop laughed heartily.

"On the contrary. The sooner you get it out of my jurisdiction, the better I like it."

DeKok pointed at the old windmill.

"Would they have heard anything, over there?"

Windt grinned.

"No, those people aren't home. Both of them left for England this week. They go there every year for Christmas and New Year. They have a son in London. The mill doesn't work anymore, you know, but I think they have plans to restore it," he added garrulously. He gestured around. "Other than them, not a soul lives along this entire stretch."

DeKok sighed, disappointed.

"So, not a chance of a witness?"

The sergeant-major grimaced.

"I wouldn't count on it," he said darkly.

Vledder returned from passing on his messages. The old police VW was parked some distance further.

"Well, I got through," he said. "We have to do something about that car, you know. And the equipment inside is just as antiquated. I could hardly make myself understood over the static."

"Were there any objections?"

"Yes, they asked why they couldn't just wait until the car was back in Amsterdam before they did the prints and the pictures. Since you're towing it anyway."

"And, what did you say?"

Vledder grinned.

"I told them that you insisted on having everything done here because of the decor."

"Good."

Vledder pointed in the direction of the VW Beetle.

"I saw a number of nice tire tracks in the soft ground over there. They seemed fresh. It seems that a car waited there for a considerable amount of time and then turned to leave in the other direction."

"The tracks don't match the ones from the Simca?"

Vledder shook his head.

"No, and they also don't look like the tracks they found in Seadike, those they found near Pete's corpse."

DeKok looked at the horizon for a long time. Then he slowly turned full circle while he looked at the scenery. The place was typical of Holland. A narrow dike with a two-lane highway on the crown, a strip of grassy clay on either side of the road surface. The road seemed to stretch on forever in either direction. Thin, almost insubstantial poplars in the distance. The water on one side and flat, unrelieved grass land on the other side of the dike. DeKok noted, but did not find it significant, that the water table was several feet higher than the land on the other side. Most of Holland was always below sea-level.

"Go ahead, Dick," he said after a long interval. "Do your measurements and so on. Make a sketch, you know what I mean. Have the photographer make a few shots of the tracks you found over there, when he shows up. Oh yes, don't forget to take some soil samples. I don't think they'll be much use, but you never know."

Vledder looked at him, surprise on his face.

"You don't want to take a closer look at the car?"

"No, not now. I want the experts to go over it first. I have a feeling about this. It seems strange, and at the same time too pat, for us to find the car now, at this late date. Just take your measurements and so on. Disturb as little as possible."

"Well, if you think so."

"Yes, I agree with the sergeant." He made a deferential bow toward the burly State cop. The gesture did not seem out of place. It was the sort of thing that one accepted as natural from DeKok. "Best wait a while with the closer examination," he continued, "the rest of them will be here soon enough."

Sergeant-major Windt looked at Vledder as he brought out his tape-measure and began.

"As for me," said Windt importantly, "I don't believe in it. In an old shed behind the post, I've got a whole pile of plaster casts of foot prints, tire prints, and you-name-it prints. I've never been able to solve even a chicken theft with it."

DeKok ignored the remarks of the State cop. He looked at his watch and wondered how much longer he had to wait before the police wrecker arrived and before the specialists made their appearance. He estimated at least another half hour.

He pulled up the collar of his coat and pushed his hands deep in the pockets. It was bitterly cold near the narrow river. There was a strong wind and even the relatively placid water between the high riverbanks showed an occasional whitecap. He paced up and down the narrow road and tried to imagine the situation when the Simca had been parked here. Why, he wondered, did they wait so long to get rid of the car? It was four days since the hold-up. Where had the car been during those four days?

Idly he watched the sergeant-major who had placed his official bicycle against a tree and was now approaching the Simca. He watched the big man come near the rear of the car and he observed how the man plucked at something green that seemed to protrude from between the lid of the trunk. The little bit of green became larger and became a green triangle. DeKok watched as if mesmerized. Windt gave a short pull and he suddenly found a hundred dollar bill in his hand.

Hastily DeKok rushed over. Without thought, almost as a reflex, he pushed the lock of the trunk. The lid flew up. Both policemen stared in consternation at the contents of the trunk. Their breath caught in their throats. In the trunk, on a thick bed of money, they found the corpse of Thornbush, the missing Secretary and Vice President of B&G.

16

A strong gust of wind dislodged some of the bank notes from under the corpse of the Secretary and pushed them along in a playful flight toward the tops of the willows. The large sergeant-major rushed after them with wide spread arms. It was a comical sight. Near the tree trunk he stopped and looked up. DeKok pressed his lips together and quickly closed the trunk before the wind could grab more money from the piles under the corpse. A single glance had been enough. Feisty Thornbush was dead, dead as a doornail. Somebody with a cynical twist of mind had placed him on top of his own loot. There was something macabre about the whole set-up, thought DeKok, something devilish. Again he realized how dangerous his prey was, how merciless

Almost in a trance, he walked away from the car and climbed the slight angle of the narrow dike. Then he stopped and looked over the situation from a distance. The various elements stood out sharply. The streamlined, blue Simca with its lugubrious cargo against the wild decor of gray, sweeping, wind-scourged clouds and deformed willows. DeKok would never forget that particular impression. Nor would he soon forget his own feeling of resignation, of despair and acceptance. The uncertain feeling, the doubt, the apprehension about the fate of Thornbush had come true. He wondered if you could have prevented it.

* * *

Traffic was slowly building up on the narrow dike. The car from the Dactyloscopic Service, the fingerprint experts, was the first to arrive. The photographer followed shortly thereafter. Next came a small wrecker from the Amsterdam Municipal Police. It was one of the type used to fish cars out of the many canals of the city. After a short interval, warned by an additional call from Vledder, an ambulance arrived, sirens blaring and lights flashing. DeKok would have preferred to see the Coroner but under the circumstances an ambulance was probably the best they could do.

After Bram, the photographer, was finished, DeKok gave the Paramedics permission to place the corpse in a body bag. He watched carefully while they lifted the corpse out of the trunk and placed it in the opened bag on the gurney.

Thornbush looked perfectly groomed. Death had not changed him much. He wore expensive shoes, a perfectly pressed, dark-blue suit and a white, silk scarf, tied like an ascot. His black, gleaming hair seemed unruffled. But a bank note had stuck to his left cheek. Just before closing the zipper of the body bag, one of the Paramedics removed it gently and replaced it in the trunk of the Simca.

DeKok gestured for them to open the zipper again. Then he called Vledder over and pointed at a pattern of hair on the coat of the dead man. The young inspector leaned forward and took one of the hairs between thumb and forefinger and inspected it carefully.

"Cat hair?"

DeKok nodded slowly.

"It looks like it. We'll double check it, of course. But considering that Thornbush is a bit of a dandy, I think the fur on his coat is a little out of place. Strange, don't you think?"

Vledder suddenly looked at him with wide eyes.

"I remember that I had cat's hair on *my* coat in about the same place, not too long ago."

DeKok grinned.

"Yes, only a few days ago. After our visit to Bent's house. They were from the black tomcat that always jumped on the laps of people when they sat in a particular chair."

"Yes." Vledder almost panted with excitement. "Yes, that's when it was." He moved his tongue along suddenly dry lips. "Do you think that . . . that Bent's place was the last place Thornbush visited before he was killed?"

DeKok looked into the distance. A sad look on his face. He visualized again the sharp features of the face he had seen near Pete Geffel's grave.

"It's possible," he said finally, reluctantly. "Of course, it's possible. But it seems a bit early to come to any definite conclusions in that respect."

Vledder looked closer at the corpse.

"How has he been killed? I don't see any wounds."

DeKok did not answer. He unbuttoned the coat of the murdered man and flipped the lapels aside. The shirt underneath and the lining of the jacket were red with blood. DeKok looked at it pensively. He lifted the arms one by one and looked at the slender hands. There was blood on the hands as well. Then he closed the dead man's coat again and motioned for the Paramedics to proceed. They zipped the body bag closed, placed the straps around the body and took off toward their vehicle.

DeKok placed a hand on the shoulder of his young colleague.

"I think I'll go with the ambulance, Dick. It seems best. The clothing on the corpse really interests me. I want to keep an eye on it. Also, perhaps I can get an autopsy today. At least I'll try." He pointed at the blue car at the bottom of the dike. "Make sure it all gets to Headquarters in one piece. And watch the money, be careful with it. Count it in the presence of others."

Vledder nodded. His face was serious.

"And what else?"

DeKok chewed thoughtfully on his lower lip. He resembled a cow chewing its cud.

"What else . . . what else? Nothing else, actually. Just make sure the money gets into the safe at Headquarters and have it sealed. Make sure somebody takes a look at the blood stains on the back seat . . . see if you can get the blood group as soon as possible."

"All right, and then?"

"Then go back to Warmoes Street and wait for me there. I think it best if we don't do anything until we've had a chance to talk. If something unexpected happens, call me. I'll be in the morgue, or at the Pathology Lab. It depends who I can snare for the autopsy."

* * *

The naked body of the late Thornbush was displayed on the black granite top of the dissecting table in the Police Pathology Laboratory. Dr. Rusteloos leaned forward and looked at the two bullet holes in the left chest. He used a probe to determine the depth of the wounds. After a while he looked at DeKok.

"At least we can determine," he remarked slowly, thoughtfully, as if begrudging every word, "that either shot would have been fatal. Of course," he added hastily, "I'll have to do a more thorough examination. It wouldn't do to be too precipitous. But for the time being, you can take that as my preliminary judgement." He paused, as if reflecting on his words, wondering whether or not he had been too positive. Then he continued:

"In any case, both shots were fired from a relatively short distance. I estimate no more than maybe four or five feet."

DeKok nodded.

"Through the heart?"

Dr. Rusteloos made a vague gesture with the hand in which he held the scalpel.

"Well," he allowed, "let's say in the region of the heart."

DeKok smiled. Sometimes Rusteloos would not even admit to the rain, afraid that the sun might shine around the corner. Nevertheless, his final reports were always accurate and very much to the point. As he said, he just did not like to be precipitous.

"Can you tell me anything about the time of death?" asked DeKok.

The doctor looked at him solemnly.

"Let's say," he answered carefully, "he's been dead between ten and twenty-four hours." He made an apologetic gesture. "You know how difficult it is to be more precise. Especially at this stage."

* * *

DeKok was sitting at his desk. The personal possessions of Thornbush were spread out before him. A white handkerchief with a discreet monogram, a comb in a leather holder, a rather small amount of money, a bunch of keys on a key ring, a plastic folder with two airline tickets to Houston, a pocket calendar and a crumpled piece of paper.

Vledder surveyed the assortment.

"Is that all?"

DeKok nodded.

"Everything he had in his pockets. I took the rest of the clothing straight to Dr. Eskes, at Forensic. I especially asked him to investigate the hair on the jacket."

Vledder picked up the crumpled piece of paper and smoothed it out with one hand, while he kept it against the desk with the other.

"Pilgrim Street," he read aloud, "number twenty-one." He frowned and looked at DeKok. "The handwriting seems familiar."

DeKok sighed.

"It's Flossie's handwriting," he said gloomily. "It's also her address." He rubbed his eyes in a tired gesture. "You know," he added, "Flossie, too, has a black tomcat."

"A tomcat?"

"Yes."

"That means that Thornbush could have picked up the hair at her place."

DeKok nodded.

"And Flossie has a clear motive," he said.

Vledder looked at him.

"Revenge?"

"Yes, she never made a secret of it. She was determined from the very beginning: She was going to punish the murderer of her fiancé. If Flossie somehow found out that Thornbush was the most likely candidate to take the 'warning' call from Pete Geffel . . . then . . . that could have been enough for her."

"Enough for murder?"

"Yes, absolutely. Flossie wouldn't have asked for any additional proof. A slight impulse, a dose of female intuition and a desire for revenge . . . and the verdict is rendered. After all, revenge is seldom the result of cool, clear thinking."

Vledder stared out of the window. He was oblivious to the noise around them. Typewriters rattled, phones rang, people were being interrogated, a door slammed and on the next desk another detective was trying to take a statement from a suspect that kept pulling on the handcuffs that secured him to his chair. But Vledder and DeKok were a little island of quiet in a sea of turmoil.

"She must have," said Vledder after a long silence, "must have enticed him to her apartment."

DeKok rubbed the bridge of his nose with his little finger. Then he stared at the finger as if he had seen it for the first time. He withdrew the finger and raised his index finger in a familiar gesture.

"What do you want? Flossie is an attractive woman, no doubt about that. And we suspect that Thornbush wasn't exactly immune to female temptations. I don't think he would have refused a direct invitation of the alluring Flossie."

Vledder smoothed the address out once more.

"And we know there was an invitation," he said pensively, "because of this note."

They both looked at the note. DeKok's face was serious and there was a strange gleam in Vledder's eyes. It was as if the small piece of paper had hypnotized them into a compelling train of thought. Vledder was the first to break the spell.

"We have to talk to her."

DeKok nodded silent agreement.

The door opened at that moment and Corporal Greanheather appeared in the doorway. He stared over the heads of the people in the room until he spotted Vledder and DeKok. Carefully he threaded his way through the crowds in the busy room. When he was next to DeKok he leaned over in a conspiratorial attitude.

"Mrs. Thornbush," he whispered. "She wants to know if you have any news about her husband."

The face of the gray sleuth fell.

"Where is she?"

The corporal waved toward the door.

"She's on the bench, in the hall. She came to the desk downstairs and asked for you. I asked her who she was. You understand, I was going to give her the brush-off. You've got enough on your plate as it is."

"And?"

"Well, of course, when she told me who she was and when she told me that you and Vledder had promised to look for her husband, well, that changed things." He made a gesture with his head and changed his tone of voice. "Isn't her husband the guy you found in the provinces?"

As a native Amsterdammer, Greanheather considered everything outside Amsterdam as the "provinces" and there was the sort of tone in his voice that suggested that if you had to get killed, Amsterdam should be good enough for anybody. No need to go out of town for that.

"Yes," answered DeKok, aware of the undercurrents in Greanheather's voice.

"Poor woman," commented the corporal.

DeKok looked at him.

"Did you tell her?"

The corporal raised both hands in the air. A gesture that suggested both outrage and denial.

"No, no," he answered hastily, "not me. That's not for me. You do it."

* * *

Corporal Greanheather guided Mrs. Thornbush across the detective room floor. DeKok quickly surveyed his desk top to make sure that all the personal possessions of her husband had been shoved into a drawer. Then he met her halfway. His face was serious as he made a slight bow. Meanwhile he watched her face carefully. Mrs. Thornbush looked pale and tired but there was a jumpy alertness in her eyes.

"Do you have news about my husband?"

DeKok did not answer. He motioned for Greanheather to leave and took her by the arm. Gently he guided her to the chair next to his desk. He placed her on the chair with the courtly formality of old-world charm, while Vledder held the chair for her. DeKok wondered how much of her behavior was due to a tightly controlled act. Mrs. Thornbush showed all the symptoms of the "broken woman" in a melodrama. It seemed too pat, too obvious. But then, some people hid their grief behind theatrics.

"Have you any news of my husband?"

There was despair in her voice.

DeKok seated himself across from her and rubbed his face with a flat hand. From between his spread fingers he looked at her and tried to gauge her inner strength. DeKok could be guilty of theatrics as well, much to Vledder's annoyance at times. This particular gesture of peeking between his fingers was so transparent that it always surprised Vledder, that few, if any people ever saw through DeKok's pretense.

"Do you have a cat?" DeKok could not have explained why he asked the question.

Mrs. Thornbush became rigid. For a few seconds she stared at DeKok with eyes that saw nothing. Then she closed her eyes and slid gracefully off the chair.

17

"And," asked DeKok with interest, "did you convey Mrs. Thornbush safely home?"

"Yes, I have."

"Did you call her physician and did you explain the situation to him?"

"Yes, yes. He would visit her immediately and he promised to keep an eye on her."

"Very well, then that's taken care of. Did she say anything in the car?"

Vledder shrugged his shoulders.

"She seemed to exhaust herself with excuses," he said cynically. "She kept harping on the trouble she had caused us. She had not meant to do it. She had never before lost consciousness, as she called it, but the emotions and tensions that had assaulted her during the recent past, had completely broken her resistance to shock."

DeKok grinned.

"Well, well," he remarked mockingly.

Vledder made an abrupt gesture.

"But not a word about her dead husband. Not the slightest manifestation of sorrow." He shook his head. "There wasn't a tear in her beautiful eyes."

DeKok smiled.

"That's not uncommon. It happens a lot. Usually the reaction doesn't set in until the full realization of the catastrophe has hit them."

"I don't know," said Vledder pensively. "I find her attitude strange, a bit weird. I would have expected her to ask all kinds of particulars. Fill her in on the details, so to speak. For instance, how her husband died and under what circumstances. I was more or less prepared for that. But nothing. Milady was too busy with herself, too full of herself. She practically wallowed in self-pity."

DeKok stood up and started to pace up and down the detective room. Whenever he passed Vledder he would toss a question, a remark, or merely a glance.

"Was there a cat?" asked DeKok on his first pass.

The young Inspector shook his head.

"I didn't see a cat. Of course, I didn't do a formal search, either. After all, I had no warrant and Haarlem is, strictly speaking, outside our jurisdiction. I just poked around a little, while Mrs. Thornbush hunted for the insurance policy on her husband. No sign of a cat. I even changed chairs a couple of times to see if I could pick up any cat hairs."

"And?"

"Nothing, no hair of any kind."

DeKok ambled over to the window and stared outside. Diagonally below him a drunk staggered from the Corner Alley, barely missed the stall of Moshe the Herring Man and half walked, half fell into the next bar. It was just one of the familiar sights from the windows of the Warmoes Street Station. How often had he stood here like this? More often than he cared to remember. How many times had he stood like this and despaired of an eventual solution? Even more times than he cared to remember.

There was no question about it. The death of Thornbush, although more or less expected, had been a shock. Of course, he had realized that the Secretary was in danger, ever since their fruitless trip to Schiphol Airport. But he had hoped, had almost been certain, that he would solve the case *before* there would be additional victims. But his thoughts had strangled themselves in a thick, sticky fog. And the mist had not cleared. His theories had become entangled in an unexpected web of intrigue that seemed insoluble. It bothered him, it tortured him, mentally as well as physically. He had the terrible feeling of having failed and his feet hurt. Whenever an investigation lacked progress, DeKok's feet would hurt. For the moment he decided to ignore it.

He turned around.

"Was Thornbush's insurance worth much?"

Vledder grinned broadly.

"Not much . . . not much at all. Certainly not enough to provide the beautiful widow with an acceptable motive."

The phone rang.

Vledder picked up the receiver and listened.

"It's for you," he said.

DeKok moved away from the window accepted the receiver from the younger man.

"Hello?"

"That you, DeKok?"

"Yes."

"All hunky-dory again?"

DeKok recognized Handy Henkie's voice.

"What do you mean?"

"Hey, with you and Lowee, of course."

179

DeKok grinned.

"You worried about that?"

"A bit."

"That's why you called?"

For a while it remained silent at the other end of the line.

"N-no . . . ," came the reluctant reply. "No . . . no I, I just wants to tell you something. You see, I just heard on the TV about the stiff you found in the province." Henkie, too, was a native Amsterdammer.

"Yes." DeKok was noncommittal.

"Well, you knows, DeKok, since I don't work because of me game leg, you see, I sometimes don't rightly know what to do with meself. I gets so bored I go visit old friends." It sounded like an apology. "You know what I means, from before. Anyways, yesterday I was with Pistol Pete . . . you knows him. Well, we're just having a few cold ones and this broad shows up. Nice looking thing, you know. Pete stashed me in another room."

"Go on."

"Well, I heard it all."

"What?"

"The chick wanted a rod."

"A rod?"

"Yessir, for real. She says she had heard about Pete and looked up his address in the phone book. I almost died laughing. Anyways, she says she lives in the provinces somewheres, real boondocks, you know. And there's this geezer that bothers her, you know. So she wants a rod to scare 'im off, so to speak."

DeKok laughed.

"Certainly a radical measure."

"Oh yes, but it weren't true, you see. It weren't no more than a story."

"How's that."

"Come on, DeKok. You could *feel* that. It were too glib, you know what I mean? She wasn't the type to be scared by men, nossir. So, I thinks to meself: why does that child need a pistol, right? Anyways, she leaves and I take off too. I follows her, you see. That weren't too easy, me with a gimp leg and all. But she was window shopping from time to time and I could catch up. So I follows her all the way."

"And?"

"She don't live in the province at all. She lives right here in town. Pilgrim Street. 21 Pilgrim Street. Leastwise, that's where she went in."

* * *

"Is this the third degree?"

She dropped into one of the low, easy chairs, crossed her long, slender legs and gave both men a challenging look. A dangerous light glimmered in her cornflower blue eyes.

"Is this an interrogation," she repeated, "or a belated sympathy visit?" Her voice dripped with sarcasm. "Just tell me what you want."

DeKok did not answer her. He rubbed his gray hair with one hand while he gestured toward the young woman with the other.

"This," he announced, "is Flossie. The lover of the late, cruelly killed Pete Geffel. I don't think you've met her before."

Vledder leaned forward and offered his hand.

"My deepest sympathy with the loss of your ... your fiancé," he said in a friendly voice. "Please believe me, I feel for you."

Ignoring his outstretched hand, she looked up at him.

"Are you another servant of the Law?" she asked mockingly.

Vledder swallowed.

"I ... I try," he stammered, "more cannot be asked of any man."

She snorted. It sounded like an insult.

"Nice platitudes to hide behind."

Vledder withdrew his hand. His face was red.

"I don't hide behind anything," he said vehemently. "Especially not behind the shortcomings of my fellow human beings. I am well aware of my own responsibility."

There was a momentary flicker of interest in her eyes, then she gave him a sad smile.

"Responsibility ... responsibility. It's a dead issue. Psychiatrists have allowed it to die and judges have helped bury it." She made a graceful gesture with her hand. "If ... you had caught the killer of my Peter, then what? Do you think he would have been punished accordingly?" She gave them a pitying laugh. "No," she continued, "no! A battery of psychiatrists with soft hands and even softer brains would have painted a picture of soul-destroying psychosis, they would have depicted the killer as a sick, deluded person." She sighed deeply. "And you can hardly expect a humane Dutch judge to send a sick man to jail, to severely punish a person who's not responsible for his actions."

DeKok looked at her, his head cocked to one side, the melancholy look on his face somehow, subtly intensified.

"And is that why ... Flossie, that's why you ... punished him?"

She did not answer. She lowered her head until her hair almost fell in her lap, she nervously adjusted the hem of her dress. The bright red color, that had marred her appearance while she was speaking, had drained from her face. She looked paler and more like the kind, nice girl so eloquently described by Mother Geffel.

"Did you punish him?" repeated DeKok.

She slowly shook her head.

"He didn't come," she answered hoarsely. "He didn't show up." She kept repeating it, like an echo, softer and farther away. "I waited all night for him," she added in a whisper.

DeKok lowered himself into an easy chair across from her.

"You had invited him?"

"Yes."

"You gave him a note with your address?"

"Yes."

"He promised to come?"

Again she nodded slowly.

"I never doubted it for a moment. I was convinced he'd show up. It wasn't until real late that I understood that someone else had gotten to him *before* me."

DeKok's eyebrows rippled briefly.

"*Before* you?"

She pushed her blonde hair away from her face and slowly raised her gaze until she looked him full in the face. A wan smile played around her lips. Then she broke eye contact.

"Men ... you men have no feelings. They've been dulled. Totally blunted. Atrophied! We women have some left. In reality we're closer to nature, the basic instinct. We have retained our animal roots since time immemorial ...

through the ages, a feeling, a feeling that warns us, prepares us and alerts us, that tells us ... without knowing."

"Intuition?"

She took a deep breath and let the air escape slowly from her lungs. It seemed an affirmation and a release.

"You *would* call it that," she answered.

They remained silent for a long time. DeKok rubbed his eyes in a tired gesture. Vledder tried to find a more comfortable place for his shoulder against the wall. Flossie remained immobile. Finally DeKok broke the silence.

"As it became later," he condensed, "and Thornbush didn't show up, you knew immediately that someone else had punished him?"

"Yes."

DeKok looked at her evenly.

"But you did invite him in order to punish him?"

Her tongue darted across dry lips.

"To kill him," she admitted softly. Her voice sounded distant, pre-occupied.

"To kill him," repeated DeKok. He leaned forward and stretched out a hand toward her. "Flossie, give me the pistol."

It seemed as if she had not heard him, as if the words broke over her like a series of sounds without meaning. She seemed far removed from what was happening in her immediate surroundings. Vledder briefly thought of the word catatonic, but then decided that her absent-mindedness was different, although not less real.

"Give me the pistol, Flossie."

DeKok's voice was friendly, but compelling.

She finally tilted her head slightly and looked at him silently. The look from her clear blue eyes was cold, chilly, without pity. Nervous tics pulled at the corners of her mouth.

Slowly the hands fell off her lap, the long fingers disappeared between the cushions of the chair, groping, feeling, touching. Suddenly, in a flash, she withdrew her hand and DeKok stared at the threatening barrel of the pistol. Her finger was around the trigger.

DeKok swallowed. He felt a rivulet of sweat drip from his head and find its way down the side of his neck. His outstretched hand almost touched the pistol. For a moment, a brief instant, he contemplated taking the weapon with a quick grab. But he remained motionless, for fear of startling her and have her fire accidentally. She could not possibly miss him at this distance.

With the utmost of self-control he caught her eyes in his gaze and he stared deep into her soul. Suddenly her face changed. The expression became milder. A faint smile appeared around the lips and reflected to a lesser degree in the eyes. For just another instant she seemed to hesitate. Then she placed the weapon into his outstretched hand.

DeKok heard Vledder's sigh of relief as if from a distance. Without looking at the younger man, DeKok knew that he was replacing his gun into the shoulder holster. Vledder had always been a quick draw and despite DeKok's disapproval of guns, Vledder seldom was without one.

DeKok looked at her empty right hand.

"Could you have?" he asked softly.

"You?"

"Yes."

"No, not you."

"But Thornbush?"

She nodded slowly, with emphasis.

"He killed my Peter."

18

"Intuition ... intuition." Vledder raised his hands in despair. "That girl makes me sick with her intuition."

DeKok laughed heartily.

"You're just upset because she wasn't impressed by you." He imitated Flossie voice, badly. "Are you another servant of the Law?" he mocked.

Vledder gestured violently.

"Law ... justice, what does that child know of either? She's so chuckfull of hate and revenge."

DeKok shook his head.

"Chockfull of sorrow," he corrected gently.

Vledder grinned deprecatingly.

"Sorrow!" he jeered. "Did you see her eyes while she was pointing that gun at you? At the slightest opportunity, at the merest excuse, she would have killed you. Believe me. And on what basis? What for? Gossip, that's all. Gossip stories from a bunch of hysterical receptionists, or whatever." His face was red with indignation. "That's all, just gossip."

DeKok rubbed his hair.

"Thornbush is dead," he remarked resignedly. "If we ever find out whether or not he killed Cunning Pete ..." He made a dejected gesture. "In any case, we can rule out Florentine La Croix as the possible killer of the Secretary. Of course, we'll go through all the routines, examine the pistol, what have you . . . But I'm almost positive that she's not responsible for the death of Thornbush."

Vledder shrugged his shoulders reluctantly.

"I'm sorry that I have to agree with you." There was regret in his voice. "I don't believe that Flossie killed Thornbush, either." He sighed deeply. "Too bad really. She would have been such a *fitting* suspect. She had a motive . . . a pistol . . . and a black cat."

With a painful expression DeKok placed his tired feet on the desk. His feet were really tired this time. Again he felt the devilish pinpricks in his calves. The pain should have abated at this stage, because he should have been closer to the solution. Instead, it seemed to have intensified. That could only mean that he was farther from a solution then he had been before. Of all his peculiarities, the feeling in his feet was the most reliable barometer of his progress. But he also hoped that this time, just this once, the feeling was a false alarm. He hoped fervently that he was closer to the end of the case then his feet wanted him to believe. He waved at Vledder who had taken a chair across from him.

"What happened to the money we found under the corpse in the trunk?"

"In the safe at headquarters."

"Has it been counted?"

"Yes, of course."

"How much was it?"

"Seven hundred and fifty thousand dollars, consisting of various denominations, but mostly American dollars. It took a lot of counting. If B&G's claim is true, we're still missing two million, two hundred and fifty thousand."

DeKok smiled.

"Plus we're missing the perpetrators."

Vledder worried for a while with his left thumbnail.

"Don't you think it's strange?" he asked after a while.

DeKok looked at him, not making the connection.

"You mean that the others took off with seventy-five percent of the loot?"

Vledder shook his head.

"No, I mean the seven hundred and fifty thousand underneath the corpse of Thornbush. It immediately raises a question."

"What question?"

Vledder made an impatient gesture.

"Why did the killer leave the money in the trunk? Nice, easy money, small bills, easy to trade ... francs ... marks ... guilders ... dollars, especially dollars. He could have spent it easily, anywhere." He banged his fist on the desk. "It's crazy. There had to be a reason."

DeKok pushed his lower lip forward.

"Perhaps," he opined, "perhaps the killer wasn't interested in the money."

Vledder stood up, agitated.

"What's the reason for this whole business?"

"Robbery," answered DeKok laconically.

"Exactly ... and why was Cunning Pete killed?"

"Most likely because, driven by the conscience *of* and his love *for* the beautiful Flossie, he wanted to prevent the hold-up."

Vledder bowed in the direction of his mentor.

"Exactly. That means that whoever organized this party, was after the money. That's all. Even a murder wouldn't stand in their way." He grinned without mirth. "And yet ... they leave seven hundred and fifty thousand bucks behind. That's tax-free, mind you. They just leave it there as a mattress for a dead Thornbush."

DeKok laughed.

"You're right, Dick. It's indeed remarkable. Highly remarkable." He moved his hands, pointed at nothing in particular. "Anyway, that car along the dike, is a remarkable situation in itself. Because of the tags we found in Farmer's Alley, we can safely presume that the car was driven there after the hold-up. But it couldn't stay there, of course. One way or the other, we would have gotten wind of a blue Simca in that neighborhood. What intrigues me, however: what happened to the car afterward? I mean what happened to the car between the time it left Farmer's Alley and until the time we found it against the willows at the bottom of the dike?"

Vledder looked for a cigarette, remembered he had given it up to please his girlfriend, and idly twirled a pen between his fingers.

"If we only knew," he remarked glumly, "who drove that car to that deserted stretch of dike, we would be a lot farther along."

DeKok nodded.

"Any luck with the tire tracks?"

"You mean the ones we found there?"

"Yes."

Vledder fished a notebook from an inside pocket.

"The soil sample," he said, searching through the pages, "is still in my desk drawer. Not much we can do with it, for now, anyway." Apparently he found the page he was looking for and folded the book inside out. "The tires," he read, "were radials and relatively new. There was a sharp, deep profile in the clay next to the road. According to those who are supposed to know, they couldn't have had more than three, or maybe five thousand miles on them. The wheelbase was almost five feet and the distance between the front wheels and the back wheels was just over ten feet."

DeKok's eyebrows danced briefly.

"What was the distance between front and back wheels?"

"More than three meters, over ten feet. It was not possible to determine the exact length. It *was* a bit slippery there, you know."

DeKok slapped himself on the forehead with a flat hand.

"I'm an idiot," he said. "I should have asked you sooner about the tire tracks."

Vledder looked at him with surprise.

"But why?"

DeKok lifted his feet from the desk and shuffled over to the coat rack.

"An overall wheelbase of more than ten feet."

Vledder followed him to the coat rack.

"What about it?"

DeKok hoisted himself into his coat.

"I'm an old-fashioned man," he grinned. "I don't know much about cars. But I do know that more than ten feet between the front wheels and the back wheels is a very long distance. Especially in Holland. People tend to use smaller cars. The average distance on the average car in Holland is maybe six to seven feet. Eight feet is probably the upper limit. Me, personally, I only know two cars with that kind of distance: a Rolls Royce and . . . a Bentley."

Vledder looked at him. For a moment he was speechless. Then his eyes glistened.

"Bent's car. Bent has a Bentley!"

With a steady hand Dick Vledder guided the police-VW through the busy traffic of the city. There was a somber, dissatisfied expression on his young face.

DeKok looked at him from aside.

"What's the matter?"

Vledder shook his head.

"Nothing," he replied, irked. "Nothing in particular. I'm just upset with myself, is all."

DeKok smiled.

"Why?"

Vledder did not answer at once. He looked straight ahead through the windshield, but DeKok had the impression that he was only partially occupied by the traffic.

"It bothers me," said Vledder after a while.

"What?"

"The tracks. The car tracks on the dike. I discovered them myself, for Pete's sake. I looked at them very carefully, I measured them. I wrote everything very precisely in my little note book ..." he did not complete the sentence.

"Well, and ..." prompted DeKok.

"Then *you* had to tell me that the tracks led to Bent ... you see, *that's* why I'm upset. I should have thought of it myself, but I never made the connection, I couldn't see the forest for the trees." He gave DeKok a suspicious look. "How," he asked, "how did you arrive at the Bentley? As far as I know, your knowledge of cars is less than my aunt's and she knows nothing at all about cars."

"It wasn't all that difficult," confessed DeKok comfortably. "It all came about because of that sergeant-major from the State Police, Windt. He said he'd never solved a case with the use of plaster casts from foot prints, or whatever. That made me think. I wondered what sort of chance *we* had under the circumstances. Our circle of suspects isn't all that great. And as far as I know, we know only positively about one car among them. And Bergen's Simca, of course. But one car stands out, is special."

"Bent's Bentley."

DeKok nodded.

"I was just idly researching some technical data on that car. You see, when he gave us a ride to his house, that was the first time I'd ever been in a Bentley. Well, that brought me to the wheelbase. It stuck, somehow."

Vledder glanced at DeKok with admiration.

"Fantastic!"

DeKok smiled.

"Thanks," he said, "but it *was* stupid not to ask you for the result of your measurements at once."

They drove on in companionable silence. They were not in a hurry, which was a good thing, because almost every traffic light was on red when they came to an intersection. After a while it started to annoy Vledder. Leaning on the steering wheel he roundly cursed the Chief of the Traffic Division who was ultimately responsible for the traffic lights. It was an unjust critique, but Vledder felt as if all the lights were deliberately set against him.

DeKok was slouched in the seat next to him. Cars were something to be endured. If it had been possible, he would just as soon have walked. But since they were driving, he felt no need to get excited about the traffic, the lights, or anything connected to this purely mechanical process. The more their progress was impeded, the more he was convinced of the soundness of walking whenever possible. Suddenly he noticed a bulge near Vledder's armpit. He stretched out a hand and felt a shoulder holster with a pistol.

"Armed?"

Vledder blushed. He felt the implied rebuke. He knew all about DeKok's abhorrence of firearms, but it was one of the few things the younger man disagreed about. DeKok felt more sympathy for the British view, which held that cops should not be armed. Vledder disagreed. Times had changed, he felt. A cop *needed* a weapon. He thought briefly about the scene with Flossie and about the two corpses they had so far encountered.

"I saw the corpse of Thornbush," he said apologetically. "I don't feel like being shot the same way, or any way, for that matter."

DeKok did not react. His thoughts were occupied by Bent. The remarks that he should never have married for a second time had taken on a deeper meaning during the course of the investigation. The wife of the B&G president was unfaithful to her husband. That much was certain. At the very least she had maintained an affair with a subordinate, with the Secretary and Vice President of the Company managed by her husband. Probably everyone, except the cuckolded husband, was aware of the situation. At least that was the usual chain of events. Was it a motive for murder? A *crime passionnel*? But what did it all have to do with the hold-up? Vledder interrupted his musings.

"You think Bent is home?"

DeKok nodded slowly.

"I think so," he said carefully. "He hasn't been in the office all day."

Vledder grinned.

"How do you know that little tidbit?"

"I had it checked, of course. You see, Bent is never long out of my thoughts. He's almost always on my mind."

"Everything is on your mind."

It sounded scornful.

DeKok shrugged one shoulder.

"I try," he said simply. "Besides, it's a matter of practice, of routine, if you will."

They passed underneath the Utrecht Bridge along the left bank of the Amstel. It was quiet. The roar of the city seemed suddenly far away. The river glistened softly in the pale moon light. It looked ghostly, ethereal. When they were near the Sorrow Fields cemetery, DeKok hoisted himself into an upright position.

"Stop here."

Vledder looked at him with astonishment.

"We're not there yet."

DeKok nodded.

"We'll walk the rest."

They parked the car near the side of the road and got out. They didn't talk while they approached the villa on foot. In front of the old house DeKok stopped and pulled a plastic bag from his coat pocket.

"Take this," he said.

"What should I do with it?"

"To keep the dirt in it, unless you want to carry it in your hands."

"Dirt?"

DeKok sighed elaborately.

"Do you remember," he asked patiently, "how we drove straight into the garage, the last time?"

"Yes."

"Fine, we'll take the same route this time, but we don't announce our visit. If Bent is home, as I expect, his car will be in the garage. You take some mud samples, some dirt, from the tires and put them in the plastic bag. I'll hold the light. Maybe we'll get lucky. It didn't rain last night and I don't think that the President cleaned his car since yesterday."

"All right, then what?"

DeKok smiled.

"Then, my friend, we will proceed to the official entrance of the residence, ring the bell and announce ourselves as honorable servants of the Law."

A broad grin appeared on Vledder's face.

"That's us," he said.

19

"Please sit down."

Bent, barefoot and wearing a camel hair dressing robe with long cords, gestured expansively toward the easy chairs in his study.

"A rather late and ... unexpected visit," said the host.

DeKok gave the man an amused look. A faint smile played around his lips. He glanced quickly at Vledder. Vledder groaned inwardly, steeling himself for another of what he called DeKok's transparent theatrics.

"Unexpected?" asked the gray sleuth, his voice trembling with sheer disbelief. "My old mother, God rest her soul, used to say: if you call for the devil ... all hell will break loose."

Vledder was puzzled, but Bent looked at DeKok for long seconds. Then he nodded.

"Your mother was a wise woman," he said.

Shyly, DeKok scratched the back of his neck.

"Yes, she was," he said dreamily. "She had the remarkable gift of understanding her fellow human beings with a single glance." He paused, as if lost in thought. Then he added: "I wonder what she would have thought of you."

"Of me?"

DeKok nodded.

"I think," he said diffidently, "that she would have said that you should never have married for the second time."

He had hit home. Bent seemed to go rigid. Color appeared in his cheeks in the form of bright, red pinpoints.

"My wife has nothing to do with it," he exclaimed, sharp and excited.

DeKok grinned.

"With what?"

The president swallowed.

"With ... eh, with the hold-up. Isn't that why you're here?"

DeKok did not answer at once. He looked at the black tomcat that was comfortably curled up and purring softly. He tried to imagine the scene of the night before. Slowly his gaze travelled through the study. The big window, the rows upon rows of books, the oak desk with the intricate carvings. No detail escaped him. Everything was exactly as during the first visit. Even Vledder was seated in the same chair.

"What are you here for?"

There was fear and suspicion in Bent's voice.

DeKok forced an expressionless face.

"We came to announce the passing of your friend, Secretary and Vice President Charles Thornbush."

"He wasn't my friend."

"You knew he was dead?"

Bent nodded slowly.

"Friends called me. It was in the news, they said."

"Was it necessary?"

"What?"

"Was it necessary for your friends to inform you?" DeKok gave him a delighted smile. "After all, you were already aware of his demise, weren't you?"

Bent's eyes narrowed. He gave DeKok a penetrating look. There was nothing but animosity in his steel-blue eyes.

"What do you mean?"

Vledder coughed discreetly, unable to keep silent.

"We mean ..." he interrupted, "that the death of Thornbush was hardly news to you. After all, you had taken your leave of him much earlier, hadn't you, at the bottom of a deserted stretch of dike?"

Bent reacted violently. Agitated, he rose from his chair. His nostrils trembled.

"I wasn't there," he screamed. "I was never there." He took a few quick, emotional steps toward the door. "I want you to leave, now. You come in here in the middle of the night and spout all sorts of indecent insinuations. What gives you the right?"

DeKok looked at him. His friendly, craggy face had changed to a look of utter astonishment.

"But we're here at your own request," he remarked apologetically. He seemed genuinely baffled.

"My request?" It was Bent's turn to display astonishment.

DeKok nodded.

"But yes. You wanted to be kept apprised of the developments in the case. You remember? Even, or so you said, if the developments would lead into a direction that would be less pleasant, even detrimental to you, or the Company."

Bent rubbed the back of his hand over dry lips. He darted nervous glances at the two inspectors. First toward one, then toward the other. He hesitated. Suddenly a cunning look came into his eyes. He walked back to his chair and sat down, calmly, outwardly relaxed.

"I had nothing to do with the death of Thornbush," he said decisively. "The news of his passing was a great shock to me too. I may add that his passing is also a great loss to the Company. Thornbush was a competent man, a trusted and loyal co-worker, who always . . ."

Vledder interrupted. He was getting angry. His eyes spat fire.

"Spare us the eulogy," he exclaimed loudly. He pressed his lips together, as if trying to bite his own words before they escaped. Then he pointed his chin toward Bent in a challenging gesture. "Or, is this a rehearsal?" His voice dripped with sarcasm. "A repetition of your speech to a willing audience of weeping willows along a forgotten stretch of the Joy." Vledder could seldom resist an attempt at alliteration.

Bent gripped the arm rests of his chair with both hands. His knuckles were white.

"I was never at the Joy," he hissed, "I told you that already."

Vledder sighed. He pulled forward a little plastic bag and held it up for all to see.

"Do you know what this is?"

"No."

"Mud . . . dirt, a soil sample. Just before we rang the bell, we scraped this off the tires of your Bentley."

Bent's intelligent face looked positively stupefied.

"My Bentley? My car?"

Vledder nodded.

"Your car, your Bentley . . . an exceptional car with an exceptional wheelbase." He smiled. "Have you ever heard of palynology? It's a scientific method to compare soil samples. It's foolproof." He gave his host a mocking look. "Am I clear enough for you? We found the tracks of your car at the Joy.

200

We took a soil sample there as well. Now do you understand, Mr. Bent? You were there. You were near the Joy."

Suddenly the company president looked ashen. The blood had drained from his face. Again he raised himself from his chair, his eyes locked onto the small plastic bag that dangled from Vledder's hand. As if dazed, as if hypnotized, he stretched out a hand to the plastic bag.

At that moment the door of the study opened and a slender woman appeared in the doorway.

"Henry!"

Her shout bounced off the walls and Bent froze in his tracks. A woman walked into the room, dressed in a clinging, turquoise nightgown made of silk. The dress whispered as she walked. She placed a hand on Bent's shoulder and pressed him back into his chair. She looked coolly at the cops.

"My husband has nothing to do with all this. You have the wrong person. I killed Thornbush."

DeKok swallowed his surprise with some difficulty.

"Y-you," he stammered, "y-you killed him?"

She nodded slowly.

"I," she said.

It seemed as if Bent suddenly recovered from his dazed state. He looked up at his wife and groped for her hand on his shoulder.

"Don't do it, Sandra," he said softly. "Don't do it."

He waved a hand at the inspectors.

"You shouldn't take her literally. She didn't really kill him. She ... eh, she ..."

Mrs. Bent lowered her head.

"I," she interrupted with a sigh, "I had an affair with Thornbush."

Her husband produced a brief, tired smile.

"Affair is too strong a term in this case," he said apologetically. "From my wife's side it was nothing more than a foolish flirtation, you understand. She never meant it seriously. You may believe me. It's really all my fault. My wife's foolishness was the result of boredom. I haven't always given my wife the sort of attention to which she's entitled. Business took too much of my time. I should have realized that a young woman . . ."

He stopped suddenly.

Mrs. Bent gave her husband a tender look. She stroked his hair in a loving gesture.

"In the beginning," she said softly, "I thought that Charles, too, I mean that Mr. Thornbush looked upon it as no more than a game, a diversion. But soon I realized that he was serious. I should have stopped it then and there. I should have told him to stay away from me. I tried, but Charles was stubborn and, I guess, determined. He kept coming, even when I made it very clear to him that I did not appreciate his visits."

She shrugged her shoulders in a sudden display of irritation. It did interesting things to her breasts that were faintly outlined under the thin material. Vledder stared, DeKok did not seem to notice.

"You see, in my heart I enjoyed it. His perseverance flattered my ego, my vanity. It gave me a strange feeling of power. I used to tease him often and perhaps my teasing enticed him even more. I don't know. I used to say that I was much too expensive a woman, that he couldn't afford me. 'Just you wait,' he used to answer, 'I'll strike it rich, one of these days. Then I'll take you with me, far away.' I used to laugh at him for that."

She paused. When she continued after a long silence, her tone of voice had changed.

"Now, yes, now I understand that I behaved like a silly goose. When I heard about the hold-up I suddenly realized what Charles had been talking about. Almost from the start I was certain that he had a hand in it. But I was afraid to say anything. I was afraid, really afraid. When you visited my husband, the other day, I hid in the bedroom. I was afraid to face you, afraid you would be able to read the guilt from my expression. Several times after that, I was on the verge of telling my husband everything. But I was afraid of that as well. I kept hoping that my feelings were wrong, that Charles had nothing to do with the hold-up." She sighed deeply. "Then I got the telephone call."

DeKok looked at her with sudden interest.

"What telephone call?"

"From Charles. He said, he said that . . ." She did not complete the sentence. She darted a haunted look at her husband. "He said," she continued, "that he had booked our flight to happiness. That's how he expressed it. He had two tickets for Houston, the first step on our way to a safe haven in South America."

"When was that?"

"Yesterday afternoon. He told me that everything had gone according to plan. He was now able to obey my slightest whim, fulfill my merest desire. I didn't have to worry about a thing. I didn't even have to bring any luggage. All I had to do was to be at Schiphol Airport on time."

"And?"

She raked her fingers through her hair.

"I . . . I didn't dare refuse."

"So you promised to meet him?"

DeKok's voice was hard and merciless.

"Yes."

"But you didn't go."

She shook her head.

"No, I didn't go. After I had replaced the receiver, after I had a chance to reflect, I suddenly realized what I had to lose. I mean, I love my husband, my house, my surroundings. To give it all up for a wild adventure with a man for whom, if truth be told, I felt nothing but a vague attraction ..."

"Go on," prompted DeKok.

"I suddenly realized how crazy it was and I realized how thoroughly I had put myself in an awkward, an untenable position. I racked my brains and finally I arrived at a solution that would rid me of him forever."

DeKok grinned broadly.

"You made an anonymous phone call?"

She nodded slowly, reluctantly.

"Yes, my husband had told me that Inspector DeKok was assigned to the investigation. I also learned where you were stationed. That bothered me for a while. You're with Homicide, aren't you?" Without waiting for an answer, she continued. "When I could not get hold of you, I left a message. Time was running out, you see."

"Thornbush," recited DeKok, "has two airline tickets for Houston, USA."

"Yes, that was the message."

"And, of course, you hoped to achieve the arrest of Thornbush *with* his loot before he could get on the plane."

"Exactly," she answered calmly. "Under the circumstances it seemed the best solution."

DeKok rubbed the bridge of his nose with a little finger. Then he looked at it as if he saw it for the first time. After a while he lowered his hand and addressed himself again to the young woman. He was struck by the pose of the couple. He, seated rigidly in his chair and she, a hand resting on his shoulder, standing proudly next to him. As if they were posing for an old-fashioned photograph. DeKok rather liked the simile. He approved of old-fashioned things.

"Did you call anyone else?" he asked finally.

She became even more rigid. With an impatient, but graceful gesture she shook the hair from her face and looked evenly at DeKok. Suspicion flickered in her green eyes.

"No," she answered emphatically. "I did not call anyone else."

DeKok made an indeterminate movement with his hand. Then he lifted a forefinger in the air.

"So, you and Mr. Thornbush were the only ones to know about the flight to Houston?"

She did not answer at once. She seemed to think about the question behind the question.

"Yes, ... eh, I assume so." She said finally. There was a distinct hesitation in her voice.

DeKok looked at her searchingly for long seconds. His sharp, trained gaze examined her facial expression. He had the feeling that she was hiding something, was keeping silent on a salient point, a point that could be very important.

Vledder showed impatience. He moved closer to the edge of his chair. In his usual, impetuous manner he broke into the conversation.

"I'm still waiting," he remarked sharply, "for an explanation of the tire tracks along the Joy."

Bent shifted his eyes to the young Inspector. Anger flashed across his face.

"My wife hasn't reached that point yet." His tone of voice matched the expression on his face. "You mustn't rush her. For the last twenty-four hours she's been exposed to inhuman stress." He rose and picked up the black tomcat. Then he led his wife to the empty chair.

"Tell them," he coaxed tenderly.

She arranged her nightgown around her.

"I was worried," she said with a deep sigh. "I could find no rest, was unable to relax. I roamed the house like a lost soul. I kept wondering if the arrest of Charles would succeed. You understand . . . the uncertainty of it all?"

DeKok nodded encouragement.

"I understand," he said, barely suppressing a smile. "If the arrest had failed, you had every reason to fear Charles, right? You were the only one who could have betrayed him."

A blush came to her cheeks.

"I'm not a stupid woman, Mr. DeKok. I have been fully aware of that danger all along. Charles Thornbush was not the sort of man who could be betrayed lightly. He would seek revenge. I didn't dare go to bed, to sleep. I kept myself awake. I waited near the phone."

DeKok's eyebrows rippled. Vledder, who had been expecting the phenomenon looked interested. Even the Bents seemed momentarily fascinated. Then, apparently deciding she could not have seen what she saw, Sandra Bent directed her attention to DeKok's question.

"Why were you waiting near the phone? What did you expect?"

"A message, news, whatever," she answered. "If you had recovered the proceeds of the hold-up, you would undoubtedly have called my husband and let him know, regardless of the time. And if the arrest had failed, I fully expected to hear from Charles. But it became later and nothing happened."

She rubbed a forearm across her brow.

"Finally, probably because of pure exhaustion, I must have fallen asleep on the sofa. After a while I woke because of a hellish noise. Still half asleep I didn't realize at once what had caused the noise. Confused I picked up the phone, but the ringing persisted. Then I realized it was the front door. I don't know how long it had been ringing before I woke up. In any case, the door bell kept ringing without interruption, as if somebody was leaning on the button. I was afraid to answer the door. I went to the bedroom and woke my husband."

Bent nodded agreement.

"The alarm clock next to my bed showed two-thirty. My wife was extremely nervous and the door bell rang as if possessed. I slipped on a robe and my wife followed me to the foyer. I switched on the outside light and opened the door. There was nobody. A broken match had been forced in next to the button and that kept it down. A few feet down the driveway was a car. A strange, blue car with the trunk wide open. I ... eh, I walked down the steps. The light from above the door reached into the trunk. Suddenly my wife was next to me. She gripped my hand and she was shaking like a leaf. We were completely at a loss, totally mystified. We were shocked. Thornbush was in the trunk ... and he was ... dead."

20

Bent pressed both hands against his face.

"It was a terrible experience," he sighed. "We must have stood there for several minutes, Sandra and I, in a complete stupor. We were absolutely stunned. When I more or less got control of myself, I went inside to call the police. My wife came after me within a few seconds. I already had the receiver in my hand and was debating between 911 and your direct number. She took the receiver out of my hands and replaced it. She asked me to first listen to her," he swallowed a lump in his throat. "Then, if I still felt like calling the police, she said I should go ahead . . ."

Again he swallowed. His eyes were moist.

"Then she told me everything . . . about her . . . game, her game with Charles . . . about the hold-up and the planned flight to Houston."

He made a helpless, sad gesture. The two inspectors listened in rapt silence and did not interrupt. After a short pause he continued.

"I don't know, Mr. DeKok, what you would have done under the same circumstances. I'm not the type to break the Law. I'm too . . . too *square* for that. Perhaps it has something to do with my upbringing. I don't know. Who knows? My name is connected to a concern that enjoys widespread trust and confidence. Although everybody calls it B&G, I never forget that it stands for *Bent* & Goossens. My great-grandfather and his friend started the business. It's a business that has been around for generations and although we have only added money transports in the last few decades, it was just a logical development. We have always transported valuable materials: museum collections of all kinds, paintings, statuary, manuscripts, instruments, you name it. If it was valuable, rare, or delicate, they'd call us to have it moved . . ." Suddenly realizing he was "making a commercial", he stopped and looked shyly at DeKok.

DeKok nodded, as if in thought. Taking heart, Henry Bent went on.

"Anyway, I thought about the articles in the papers, on TV, in magazines. I thought about the tens of thousands of small investors and our employees. I reflected that you had been looking for the guilty party *within* the Company, almost from the beginning. And then, a dead Thornbush in front of my own house . . ."

He was unable to go on. DeKok came to the rescue. He nodded understandingly with a friendly expression on his face.

"You decided the corpse had to disappear."

Bent reached for a pack of cigarettes on the table with hands that shook almost uncontrollably. When he finally had managed to pick it up he held it in his hands, as if it were a security blanket.

"Yes," he said after a while, "he had to go. I dressed quickly and went back outside. Only then, to my surprise, I discovered that it had to be the blue Simca that was, according to reports, involved in the hold-up. There were stacks of bank notes under the corpse. But I wasted little

210

time on that. I closed the trunk and searched the car. The hood was still warm. It could not have been there very long on a cold night like that. I tried the doors. They were not locked. The key was still in the ignition. I sat down behind the wheel, turned the key and the engine started immediately. I went back inside and told my wife to follow me in the Bentley, preferably at some distance. I wanted to avoid looking like a procession, you see, tried to avoid curiosity."

He paused again. Vledder made a movement as if to say something, but DeKok restrained him with a silent glance. The young man sank back in his chair, content to take his lead from DeKok. DeKok also sat in silence. Mrs. Bent moved slightly in her chair, but made no attempt to add to her husband's narrative. With an effort, Bent seemed to return to the present. He sat up a little straighter and spoke again.

"At that time I had no idea what to do with the car." His voice had become firmer, more decisive. "I drove along the Amstel toward Oldwater. Then across the bridge in the direction of Utrecht. Then I thought about the Joy. I had driven past that particular spot a number of times in the past. Not many people know it's an excellent short-cut between Amsterdam and Utrecht. You avoid all the traffic. I remembered particularly the stretch near the old mill. It seemed the ideal spot to abandon the car."

DeKok nodded.

"Especially near the old, weeping willows."

Bent shook his head sadly.

"Believe me, the surroundings had nothing to do with it, although the place *does* remind one of a cemetery. But I don't have an eye for that sort of detail. To me it was just a deserted spot, hard enough to come by in our country. I wanted to get rid of the car with its hideous cargo. That's all. The Joy was a subconscious choice."

DeKok could almost feel the relief in the man, now that he had apparently told it all. He changed the subject of the conversation to something more germane, something that interested him more than the actual scene that had left such a vivid picture in his mind.

"You pushed the car off the road, down the embankment until it rested against the trees." His voice was matter-of-fact, business-like. "You wiped off the fingerprints that you might have left and got out of the car. Then you stepped into the waiting Bentley with your wife and, no doubt greatly relieved, drove home."

Bent smiled bleakly.

"Relieved . . . I've never in my life felt as bad, as . . . as threatened, as then."

Vledder could not contain himself any longer. His youthful impetuosity took control of his actions, made him appear heartless. He laughed derisively.

"Come, come, Mr. Bent," he said contemptuously. "You had every reason to be proud of yourself . . . you had just gotten rid of a annoying co-respondent, a competitor for your wife's love."

Bent's face became red. If looks could have killed, Vledder would have been dead on the spot.

"That . . . that," he stammered in his anger, looking for words, "that's a . . . a highly . . . disagreeable remark."

Vledder grinned broadly.

"Murder is a highly disagreeable crime."

Bent jumped up from his chair.

"I didn't kill Thornbush," he screamed at the top of his voice. Startled, the tomcat jumped from his arms and landed gracefully on the floor. "I tell you, he was dead already!"

Vledder looked up at him, a taunting look in his eyes.

"Really, Mr. Bent, please be serious. Surely you didn't expect for a moment that we would believe your story. I mean: finding the Simca in front of your house and your wife's ex-lover as cargo. It defies rationalization."

Vledder's voice became more and more sarcastic. His attitude more pugnacious. DeKok watched carefully. Vledder was a young man with a mercurial temperament at times. A sharp mind, but an impetuosity barely kept in check by better judgement.

"I'll tell you what really happened," said Vledder sharply. "When Thornbush realized that his paramour did not arrive at the airport on time, he came to get her. You received him in a friendly manner and courteously led him to this room. Then you told him that Milady had changed her mind. It was over. But determined Charles didn't take no for an answer. He had risked everything for his love, burned all bridges behind him. He wasn't about to give up now. He insisted that you immediately relinquish your hold on your wife, Mr. Bent. Consequently you saw but a single solution . . ."

The cat raised his head and miaowed for attention. When Vledder glanced at him, he jumped up and nestled himself comfortably on the Inspector's lap. The couple looked on as if mesmerized.

Vledder gently stroked the soft fur of the black tomcat. His motions were slow, barely kept in check by an enormous inner tension. Slowly he looked up at Henry Bent. The look in his blue eyes was as cold as ice, but he became calmer, less vehement, as if the cat had a therapeutic effect.

"You forgot the cat hairs," announced Vledder softly.

* * *

They drove back to the city along the banks of the Amstel. The engine of the old VW sputtered and the rusted exhaust added additional noises. The racket echoed across the water.

Vledder kept his eyes on the road. He looked pale and there was a tired look on his face.

"I do believe," he remarked thoughtfully, "that we should have arrested those two."

DeKok ignored the remark with supreme indifference.

"It was a wonderful theory," he said instead, with admiration in his voice. "And so convincingly performed. If Mr. and Mrs. Bent had indeed killed Thornbush in conjugal cooperation, then they would most certainly have confessed after your accusation." He produced an embarrassed smile. "You even had me wondering there, for a while."

Vledder gave his old partner a quick look. There was a question on his face.

"You mean to tell me you *believe* the story they dished up?

DeKok shrugged his shoulders nonchalantly.

"I have no reason to *dis*believe it. It is entirely possible that the Bents are not responsible for the death of Thornbush. It is entirely possible that the real killer did indeed park the car with the corpse in front of their door."

Vledder shook his head in despair at so much obtuseness.

"But who? And why?"

DeKok released a deep sigh.

"I hope to get an answer to both questions before the night is out."

"Tonight still?"

DeKok looked at his watch. The old VW did not even have such a minimal convenience as a dashboard clock.

"It's half past midnight. You better hurry. We only have another half hour."

Confused, Vledder looked at him.

"Half an hour? What for?"

"To arrest Little Lowee."

"Little Lowee?"

There was incredulity in Vledder's voice.

DeKok nodded slowly, pensively.

"Yes, during the week he closes his bar at one in the morning. Usually it's packed toward that time. I know that from experience. And I want you to arrest Lowee in front of all his clientele. Half the neighborhood will be there, you see. You understand? I want you to make a big production out of it. Take all the uniforms you can find with you. For all I care, you order a Paddy Wagon. But be loud about it, make a fuss, be obvious. Make sure everybody hears that Lowee is being arrested for complicity in a hold-up, that he's responsible for . . . for the murder of Pete Geffel."

Vledder looked at him with wide eyes.

"But . . . but that's a lie!"

DeKok grinned cheerfully. His melancholy face lit up with a boyish delight.

"Yes, indeed, a barefaced lie."

21

Little Lowee looked the worst for wear. Apparently he had forcefully tried to resist arrest. His black necktie now hung on his back and part of his shirt hung out of his trousers. He wiped the sweat off his face with the sleeve of his torn jacket.

"Seeing as we've known each other for so long," he spat, "I woulda thought you'd come yourself and not send one of your errand boys. Whatsa matter, was you scared to do your own dirty work?" He snorted in disgust. "And all that brouhaha. Half the Quarter was in uproar. You couldn't walk for the cops. The streets were almost blue with 'em. Dammit, I ain't Al Capone."

DeKok glanced at Vledder who made some notes at the next desk. For once it was relatively quiet in the detective room. Just one other plain clothed man was working on something or other at the far side of the room.

DeKok returned his gaze to Little Lowee and waited calmly until he finished venting his anger. He understood full well why the slender barkeeper was so upset. He would much rather have taken a different course of action himself, but time was pressing. He could not afford to wait any longer.

When the stream of invective finally dried up, DeKok carefully placed his elbows on the desk, folded his hands underneath his chin and looked at Lowee with a smile on his face.

"I don't even need you."

It sounded especially laconic and took Lowee's breath away.

Lowee swallowed.

"But that's false arr. . ."

DeKok raised a restraining hand.

"Please understand me. I do have formal grounds for keeping you here several hours. But I don't want you at all, at all."

"Don't want me?"

DeKok shook his head.

"I want the boys from the hold-up."

Lowee looked at him in surprise.

"And for that you up and arrest me?"

DeKok nodded slowly.

"With, as you said, a lot of brouhaha. I wanted everybody in the neighborhood to know that Little Lowee had been arrested and taken to Warmoes Street. And I wanted to make sure that everybody knew it was for the hold-up and . . . the murder of Pete Geffel." He pushed his lower lip forward. "You see, I know my customers. I'm sure that somebody is informing the guys at this very moment."

Lowee looked at the Inspector with suspicion in his eyes.

"So what?"

DeKok grinned in a friendly way.

"So, then I expect them to come forward to tell me something I have known all along . . . that you had nothing to do with the hold-up, or the murder."

The barkeeper nodded understanding.

"I'm the bait."

"More or less." DeKok sighed deeply and changed his tone of voice. "I've always liked you Lowee," he said earnestly. "And I've always appreciated you. Still do. There's few like you. You're honest."

The barkeeper grimaced.

"Big deal. That and a quarter don't even get me a cuppa coffee."

DeKok ignored the remark.

"When you," he continued unperturbed, " didn't want to give me the names of the boys . . . not even after I dragged you to Pete's funeral, I figured you didn't do it necessarily for profit. You had to be convinced that the guys you protected were innocent of Pete's death." He made a gesture with a hand that seemed to say it all. "Otherwise you would never have helped them and you would never have kept your mouth shut." He paused again and scratched the back of his neck. He looked embarrassed. "Actually," he added, "your attitude toward those boys is the real reason for your arrest."

"What?"

"I'm speculating on your ability to judge people."

Lowee slapped his narrow chest in utter astonishment.

"My . . . what?"

DeKok nodded.

"Yes, if you have gauged the guys correctly, if you think they are really 'trustworthy', then they'll give themselves up, rather than see an innocent person suffer for their crimes. They'll want to protect you from 'the jaws of justice', you see?"

"Me?"

"Yes."

"And what iffen they sees right through you? What then, you clever dick?"

DeKok spread his arms wide in a gesture of surrender.

"I give them three hours. If they haven't given themselves up in that time, I let you go."

The phone on his desk rang at that moment. DeKok lifted the receiver and listened. Little Lowee looked intently at the face of the Inspector, trying to guess what the conversation was about. But DeKok's poker-face did not change. It remained even, expressionless. A steel mask.

After a few seconds DeKok replaced the receiver. Slowly he rose from his chair and waved toward the door.

"Put your shirt back into your pants, straighten your tie and leave. You're free to go."

For just an instant the barkeeper hesitated, then he stood up and left the detective room without another word. DeKok accompanied him part of the way.

"Don't poison my cognac, tomorrow."

The answer was lost in the sound of the slamming door.

* * *

"I heard you arrested Little Lowee."

DeKok stared into the friendly open face of a tall, somewhat awkward young man.

"That is correct."

The young man smiled shyly.

"I came to tell you that Little Lowee wasn't part of the hold-up. He also knows nothing about Pete Geffel's murder."

DeKok nodded with pursed lips.

"That," he said, "is an extremely clarifying announcement."

The young man cocked his head to one side and pulled on his left earlobe.

"Lowee is innocent. I know that."

"So?"

"Yes, my brother and I committed the robbery. We're guilty. We held up the money transport."

DeKok did not react immediately. His sharp gaze travelled from the open sandals and baggy pants to the red corduroy jacket with leather patches on the elbows. He studied the full mouth and the weak chin and questioned seriously how this friendly personality could have committed an armed robbery. He looked too guileless, almost artistic.

"You and your brother?"

There was a distinct tone of suspicion in his voice.

The young man nodded.

"My brother conveys his regrets. He wanted to come along, but he was unable to do so. He's in bed and still very weak. A rather disreputable, but obviously competent person *did* take two bullets out of his back." Again he gave DeKok a shy smile. "One of your people found it necessary to shoot at us," he added.

DeKok made an apologetic gesture.

"After all, you *did* find it necessary to be armed when you robbed the transport." He smiled. "How is your brother?" There was warm interest in his voice.

The young man pushed his hair out of his eyes.

"Now that the bullets have been removed, he's fast improving. Not in small part because of Little Lowee's assistance, I might add. We owe him a lot. Lowee is one in a thousand."

DeKok nodded slowly.

221

"I know," he said resignedly. "His arrest was a mistake, a psychological blunder. Therefore I released him immediately."

Something flickered momentarily in the young man's eyes.

"Released?"

DeKok looked at him, a question in his eyes.

"Isn't that what you wanted?"

The young man nodded emphatically.

"Indeed, yes. That's why I came. As soon as my brother and I heard about his arrest, we knew it was our duty to report in."

"And the third man?"

For the first time the young man showed a serious expression. The boyish appearance left his guileless face.

"There was no third man."

DeKok's eyebrows vibrated like the antennae of an insect. Both Vledder and the young man took a sudden interest in the phenomenon. As usual, DeKok was totally unaware of the effect. His eyebrows did seem to live a life of their own.

"That's strange," remarked DeKok. "Three people were observed. There's no doubt about that."

The young man shook his head, unable to tear his gaze away from DeKok's forehead.

"There was no third man."

DeKok sighed elaborately. His eyebrows subsided.

"Who," he asked patiently, "got out of a blue Simca behind the Central Station and threatened the guards with weapons?"

"My brother and I."

DeKok grinned. For a moment it looked like the young man would grin in return at the irresistible charm DeKok displayed at such moments. Then he took note of DeKok's words.

"Who was the third man, behind the wheel?"

The young man bowed his head.

"We . . . eh, my brother and I," he said softly, hesitating slightly, "my brother and I have decided to take full responsibility."

"Responsibility for what?"

"For the robbery and . . ." his voice broke for a moment. He bit his lower lip and then uttered: ". . . and the murder."

"What murder?'

"The murder of Pete Geffel."

DeKok's mouth compressed into a narrow, implacable line.

"Who put the dagger in his back?"

The young man tried to escape the hard eyes of the Inspector. His hands started to shake and his lips trembled.

"It . . . eh, it was *my* dagger."

DeKok banged his fist on the desk in a sudden display of anger.

"That's not what I asked," he roared. Then, in a normal tone of voice he repeated the question. "I asked who put the dagger in Pete's back. Who stabbed him."

The young man swallowed.

"I . . . I did it, I stabbed him."

The gray sleuth dropped back into his chair. He rubbed his eyes in an infinitely weary gesture. He looked at the young man.

"You know," he said, shaking his head, "I don't believe you. Nossir, I don't believe you at all, at all."

The young man smiled.

"You have little choice, I think. You have two options. You may believe me, or . . . not. I can assure you that my

223

brother will tell you exactly the same thing." He made an abrupt, meaningless gesture. "But why should you worry about it? Don't search for answers that aren't there. The case is closed, solved. You know who killed Pete Geffel and you know who did the hold-up. You can consider it solved, close the file and forget it. From our side we will promise you solemnly that we will stick to our story to the bitter end." He spoke as if he was explaining some elaborate practical joke instead of a serious crime.

DeKok looked at him in total astonishment. Again he studied the face. The full lips, the blond hair, the green eyes. Suddenly something clicked. It was as if the veils had been ripped away from his eyes, as if his brain was suddenly allowed to run again at full speed with a new infusion of oxygen. Suddenly it was all clear to him. He stood up and forced his face into the friendliest of smiles.

"I must correct an oversight," he said cheerfully.

"An oversight?"

DeKok nodded.

"Yes, it's really unforgivable. I never did introduce myself." The gray cop stretched out his hand in an inviting gesture and announced:

"My name is DeKok, with . . . eh, kay-oh-kay."

The young man rose slowly from his chair. He took the hand and said:

"I'm Tim . . . Tim Klarenbeek."

* * *

Considering the lateness of the hour, Mrs Thornbush looked extremely well groomed. It seemed as if she had expected the visit from the two Inspectors and had prepared herself for it. The blonde hair was put up in a complicated style and her make-up was flawless. The light purple duster she wore did nothing to conceal her attractive shape, instead seemed to accentuate it. She was seated in a wide, easy chair covered with an off-white material. She had tucked her legs under her on the chair and now she gestured at DeKok with a pale hand.

"Can you tell me who killed my husband?"

DeKok looked at her. There was a slight vibration in her voice, a slight undertone that indicated fear and uncertainty. It was in complete contrast to her relaxed, somewhat arrogant posture.

"Is that what you expected?'

She smiled.

"Isn't that what the police is for? To solve murders and other nasty things like that?"

DeKok nodded.

"Indeed," he drawled, "that's what the police is for." He rubbed his face as if thinking about the next words. "Actually," he went on in the same lazy, slow tone of voice, "the police are very irritating people. They're always sticking their noses where it isn't wanted and they always want to know the how, what and wherefore of everybody's business." He grinned shyly, as if apologizing. "Yet, despite all that rooting around, many cases remain completely unsolved, remain unexplainable. The real motives can seldom be identified." He gestured in her direction. "You should understand . . . I know why your husband was killed . . . but I don't understand your husband."

The corners of her mouth trembled.

"You know why my husband was killed?'

"Yes."

She frowned. There was an alert look in her eyes.

"Then . . . what is it you don't understand?"

DeKok looked at her evenly.

"Why he longed for another woman."

The remark hit like a bolt of lightning. Suddenly she lost her pose and her poise. The alluring impression melted away. She jumped up like a banshee, her face transformed by hate.

"Because . . . because . . ." She caught herself suddenly. Within fractions of a second she again had herself under control. She wiped the look of hate from her face and smiled wanly, without joy. A smile that went no further than her lips.

"Some men are insatiable in their desires." It sounded like an apology. "They simply have too much love for just *one* woman."

"That, in itself," said DeKok thoughtfully, "was not enough reason to murder him, Mrs. Thornbush. You had known for some time that he was cheating on you."

It was a second attack on her equanimity. She rose above it. She closed her eyes, sat down and lowered her head as if overcome by grief and weariness.

"I . . . eh, I had gotten used to the idea," she whispered. "I had learned to live with it."

DeKok nodded.

"Until he betrayed you."

She looked at him. The corners of her mouth trembled. Her lower lip dropped slightly.

"I don't know what you mean."

It was a pathetic attempt at denial, a feeble defense.

DeKok pressed his lips together.

"Where's the money?"

An angry, malicious flicker in her eyes broke through her mask of confused innocence.

"What money?"

DeKok grinned ruefully.

"The money from the hold-up. Two million, two hundred and fifty thousand to be exact."

She looked at the Inspector with unconcealed hostility.

"I don't have it."

DeKok gestured vaguely around.

"I have reasons to believe it's in this house. I suggest you voluntarily give us permission to search." He spoke in a friendly, convincing tone of voice while he gauged her possible reaction. "It saves time," he continued, "and we'll find it anyway."

For a few seconds she seemed undecided. Then she slipped out of the chair and walked to a sideboard.

"You won't find it."

The threatening tone in her voice should have warned the gray sleuth, but for once he was too certain, too overly confident.

He tapped Vledder on the shoulder.

"Go look, Dick," he said. "Start with the garage. I think I saw a connecting door from the kitchen."

Vledder took a few steps in the direction of the corridor.

"You're not going to the garage."

It sounded like an order.

Completely taken aback both cops turned around to look at the woman. She was leaning against the sideboard and there was a pistol in her right hand.

The confusion on Vledder's face was quickly replaced by a mocking smile. Challenging her, daring her, he took a step in her direction.

There was the sudden explosion of a shot.

22

DeKok strode down the long corridor of the hospital with an unfamiliar shopping bag filled with fruit awkwardly under one arm. A blushing nurse pointed the way.

Vledder looked pale, even against the white hospital sheets. His face still bore traces of pain and emotion. But a smile appeared on his lips when he spotted DeKok. His stumbling, cumbersome entrance, combined with the worried look on his face were positively comical to his young partner.

The gray sleuth made quite a production of depositing his old, decrepit hat at the foot of the bed. Then he pulled up a chair and sat down.

"I . . . eh, I brought you some oranges and stuff," he said with a helpless gesture. "I hope you like it. I don't know what they feed you in this place."

"Thank you," answered Vledder. DeKok was from a generation that equated hospital visits with fruit baskets.

DeKok placed the bag next to Vledder.

"How is it going?" he asked, concerned.

Vledder pointed toward his shoulder.

"They took the bullet out. There it is, on the night table, in the tube."

DeKok took the bullet from the medicine bottle and let it roll over the palm of his hand.

"The same caliber that put an end to Thornbush?"

Vledder nodded. His face was serious.

"Yes, his wife killed him."

"That's right, Dick, and she almost killed you as well. We finished the interrogation this afternoon. She confessed fully and in detail."

Vledder shook his head in confusion.

"It's terrible," he sighed. "Just terrible. Despite the fact that she fired at me, tried to kill me, I still think it's terrible."

DeKok looked at him with considerable surprise.

"Why?"

"I liked her. She seemed such a dear . . . *sweet* woman. The last thing I expected was that she would actually pull the trigger. I just didn't think her capable. Despite your hints about her being responsible for the death of her husband, I just couldn't accept it intellectually. Naive, I suppose."

DeKok pulled on his lower lip and let it plop back. He did that several times. It was an annoying sound, one of his more irritating habits.

"Yes," he said after a while, as if reminiscing. "Yes, soft and sweet. She *used* to be just that. Before Thornbush woke the devil in her and drove her to murder."

Vledder frowned.

"Thornbush drove her to murder?"

DeKok nodded.

"Yes, he drove her to kill him." He moved in his chair, trying to find a more comfortable position on the unyielding hospital furniture. "Perhaps I should tell the whole story. You should be strong enough, by now. Besides . . . you're entitled to know."

Vledder smiled.

"Tell me already."

DeKok rubbed his face with a flat hand.

"Some people," he began slowly, "are driven by dreams. Charles Thornbush dreamed about a carefree existence in South America with the woman he loved at his side."

"Mrs. Bent."

"Yes, he had maintained a more or less intimate relationship with her for some time. His wife knew about it. He never even bothered to keep it a secret from her. He admitted to her, on several occasions, that he was fascinated with Bent's wife. Mrs. Thornbush accepted it, endured it, because she really loved her husband deeply. She hoped passionately that his infatuation with the other woman would be a temporary thing."

"But it wasn't."

DeKok shook his head slowly, sadly.

"No, Thornbush was possessed. He was driven by his dream. About three months ago he came up with a plan. You'll remember that Mrs. Thornbush's maiden name was Klarenbeek. Well, she has two brothers: Tim and Walt Klarenbeek. The boys are a bit bohemian and have a friendly, cheerful, casual attitude to life. They both have some artistic talent that affords them a reasonable living. They have a studio in some basement near the Front Fort Canal. One of them paints a bit and the other does weird things with metal, mobiles, I think you call them."

He paused briefly, looked worriedly at Vledder and asked him if it was not too tiring for him. Upon Vledder's denial, he continued.

"Well, whenever they needed some extra cash, they would do something commercial, design stands for exhibitions, or what have you. Their output wasn't great, but it was enough. They really couldn't care less. They had enough to eat for their needs and an extra beer whenever they wanted. Besides, Little Lowee had a weak spot for them and would often draw them free beer. If they really were short, they could always tap their 'bourgeois' sister in Haarlem for some extra cash. After all, Thornbush made good money and he would never notice the amount."

Again he paused briefly.

"Anyway," he went on, "during one of their expeditions for extra cash, Thornbush revealed his plans and enlisted their help."

"The hold-up?"

"Exactly. It was really very simple. Thornbush travelled extensively for the firm. He had picked up a couple of pistols somewhere. You know how it's almost impossible to obtain handguns in Holland. But now, with the EEC and all, it's very easy to bring them into the country. Nobody checks luggage anymore, especially on trains."

"I know," remarked Vledder. "Last year Celine and I went to Spain. I could almost have left my passport at home. You just hold it up as the Customs people pass through the train. The cover is enough."

"Right," agreed DeKok. "Anyway, it was thought that the guards would be so frightened at the mere sight of the pistols, that they would cause no problem. There was virtually no risk. They simply had to wait for the right transport. Thornbush, because of his job, would know exactly when that would happen. He would also know the route, of course. The boys were immediately in favor of the plan. After all, so they reasoned, nobody would get hurt. The company was insured and as for the insurance company . . . well, insurance companies made too much money anyway."

He shook his head, reached over to the bedside table and took a large sip of Vledder's water.

"Mrs. Thornbush didn't like it, didn't agree at all. It was criminal, she said and she was especially upset about the involvement of her two younger brothers. That's when Thornbush played his ace in the hole." Again he shook his head. "Are you sure you're all right?" he asked. "I really don't want to tire you, you know."

"No, no, I'm fine," said Vledder impatiently. "Now that I know most of it, I want to know the rest. Don't forget, after I stopped that bullet, I was out of it for all practical purposes. I'm better off knowing. Don't keep me in suspense."

"Well, all right." It sounded dubious. "As I said, he played his ace card. During some pillow talk he had confided to his wife that he had tried to break the relationship with Sandra Bent. He told her that he finally realized that she couldn't possibly compare to his own wife. But, he asserted, Sandra didn't want to hear about a break. She insisted that he keep the relationship going. She had, according to Thornbush, threatened to ruin his standing at B&G. She had ways to influence her husband, she said. Then he added that the money could make them financially independent and they could all go to South America together, far away from the pernicious influence of his boss' wife."

"And?"

"Mrs. Thornbush gave in. She even insisted on taking an active part in the hold-up. They agreed that she would dress as a man and she would drive the getaway car."

"So, there was your third man."

DeKok nodded pensively.

"Yes. The first attempt failed because of a mistake by Walt. During a rehearsal he was so nervous that he promptly put the stolen car against a light pole. He was just as promptly arrested and disappeared for a month. He served his sentence in the Haarlem jail."

Vledder's eyes lit up.

"And that's where he met Pete Geffel."

"Yes. They vaguely knew each other from their visits to Little Lowee's ... eh, establishment. In jail they became better acquainted with each other and Walt Klarenbeek told Pete in a confidential mood about his glorious plans for a hold-up. For one reason or another he kept silent about the role of his brother-in-law, the VP. No doubt in order to impress his underworld acquaintance he emphasized his own role in the plans. He just mentioned in passing a contact within the company that knew all about the money transports."

DeKok stopped and for a long time he stared at nothing in particular.

"Fate took a hand at that time," he said somberly, "the cards were dealt and the game would be played to its inevitable end. It's a sad fact that it was actually Flossie who started the ball rolling. She forced Peter to inform the company."

"And Pete landed in the not-so-tender hands of Thornbush."

DeKok nodded.

"I've been wondering how Cunning Pete could have fallen so naively into the trap that Thornbush had set him. One explanation is that Pete just wasn't himself. His entire life he had dealt in cheating and lying. He had concentrated on the seamier side of 'business', so to speak. He just wasn't prepared to deal in an atmosphere of openness and honesty. Thornbush exploited that very cleverly. It's possible that Thornbush promised him some sort of reward. We'll never know. No matter, he succeeded in enticing him to the sand dunes and slipping a dagger into his back."

Vledder gestured with his left arm.

"But Tim said it was *his* dagger and *he* had done the stabbing."

DeKok smiled.

"Tim has retracted that confession. As soon as he realized that I was aware of his sister's role in all this, he became more forthcoming. The dagger was an old family heirloom. The boys had it on the wall as a decoration. On the afternoon after the hold-up, Thornbush visited them in their hideaway in Farmer's Alley. He scolded Walt for his loose lips in jail and then added, calm as you please, that he had been forced to silence Cunning Pete forever. Both boys were furious and threatened to inform the police. Thornbush advised them differently. In the first place, so he said, their sister would not escape punishment as an accomplice in armed robbery and as far as the murder was concerned ... that was committed with an antique dagger of a special design. Only then did the boys realize that the dagger had been missing for some time."

"What a bastard."

Vledder's voice trembled with indignation.

DeKok looked searchingly at his younger colleague. There was an unhealthy, excited blush on his cheeks.

"I really think I better stop," he said, genuinely concerned. "I'll let you know the rest some other time. This cannot be healthy for you." He groped for his hat and showed every indication of leaving.

Vledder pushed himself up on his left elbow, a painful grimace on his face.

"If you stop now," he threatened, "I'll get out of bed and follow you until I know it all."

DeKok nodded.

"Blackmail," he said resignedly.

Vledder grinned.

"Call it what you will."

DeKok sighed ostentatiously.

"All right," he said with uncharacteristic meekness, "what else do you want to know?"

Vledder shook his head in frustrated despair.

"Everything, of course. For instance, what led you to suspect Mrs. Thornbush? I don't recall anything that pointed in that direction."

DeKok grinned.

"Mrs. Thornbush made a small mistake. When she went to Farmer's Alley to visit her brothers, the day after the hold-up, she didn't know that Little Lowee had taken the boys to a new hiding place. Much to her surprise and shock she was suddenly attacked by us. In order to explain her presence she said that she had found the address in her husband's pocket calendar. You see, that aroused my suspicion. A businessman, certainly a VP and Secretary of a large company, doesn't usually leave the house without his appointments. When we found him later, near the Joy, his note book was in his pockets. You may remember that I went through it, page by page. The address in Farmer's Alley wasn't there."

Vledder smiled.

"So, obviously she lied and knew more about the hold-up and the robbers than she let on."

"Exactly. Therefore there was every reason to keep an eye on Mrs. Thornbush. When she came to the station, supposedly to inquire about her husband, she fainted when I asked her about a cat. In view of the cat's hair on the corpse's clothes, it reinforced my suspicion that she knew *something* about the death of her husband. That's why I had you drive her home. Then, when you returned and reported that you had seen nothing of a cat, I was momentarily at a loss. It seemed a dead end. But not for long. The story from the Bents about the Simca, the money and the dead Thornbush, brought the trail right back to her."

Vledder looked at him with a confused look on his face.

"I don't understand that."

"You remember what you said when we found the corpse? Why did the killer leave the money in the trunk. Tax-free money, you said."

"Yes."

"It was a good question, but the thrust of the question was wrong."

"How's that?"

"We should have asked ourselves why whoever killed Thornbush placed the body on a bed of bank notes. And not just a quantity of bank notes, but *exactly* seven hundred and fifty thousand dollars, or the equivalent, anyway."

"You mean that the amount had a certain significance?"

"Yes. We even touched upon it, briefly. We mentioned that seventy-five percent was still missing. You see, that was crucial. It meant that exactly twenty-five percent was in the trunk. You understand? Thornbush had been placed on top of *his* share."

Vledder beamed.

"Dammit, yes. From that it followed that there *had* to be three others."

DeKok nodded.

"But not just that. It also meant that in killing Thornbush, other motives, besides money, were a consideration. Under normal circumstances, any gang of four, would have divided the spoils into three after the demise of one of their members. But that didn't happen. Charles Thornbush received his full share. He *and* his share were then transported to the villa at the Amstel, to the Bent house. Why? As we know now, Bent had nothing to do with the entire mess. But Sandra Bent was a different kettle of fish altogether. She was presented with her lover, complete with his share of the loot . . . but he was dead as a doornail."

DeKok rubbed his eyes with the back of hand.

"That type of cynicism could only be conceived by the brain of a jealous woman."

His voice sounded bitter. For a long time after that they remained silent. Wet snow was sticking to the outside of the window. Vledder was the first to break the silence. There was a deep crease in his forehead, something that usually happened when he concentrated deeply on something.

"But I don't understand how she could kill her husband. After all, she *did* love him very much. What was the direct cause for that?"

DeKok sighed.

"She found the tickets for Houston."

"What?"

"Yes. Tim had told her about the dagger and the murder of Pete Geffel. From that moment on she looked at her husband with new suspicion. She followed him unobtrusively and discovered that he had plans to abscond with the entire loot. When she then, more or less by accident, found the airplane tickets she suddenly realized the how and the why of the entire plan. She realized that she had been lied to and that she and her brothers had been used in order to enable him and his paramour to flee to South America. That was too much, that was the straw that broke the camel's back, so to speak. She took one of the weapons that had been used during the hold-up and waited for him in the hall. In her heart she doubted herself. She did still have a faint hope that she was mistaken. She hoped that, perhaps, the second ticket was for her. But Thornbush ignored her, didn't even notice her in the hall. At the moment that he was about to leave with his suitcases, she called him back and shot him from close by."

DeKok rose from his chair and ambled through the room. There were two other beds, but both were unoccupied. He stopped in front of one of the windows and stared at the snow. Vledder looked at his broad back.

"Did you find the missing money in the garage?"

"No, not in the garage, but in suitcases under the bed."

"Not in the garage?" asked Vledder, astonished at the revelation.

DeKok turned toward him.

"No."

Vledder swallowed.

"But . . . but, then *why* did she shoot me when I wanted to go to the garage?"

"The cat was there."

"The cat?"

DeKok nodded slowly.

"Thornbush also had a cat, from before his marriage. But Mrs. Thornbush didn't like cats, is allergic to them. The animal wasn't allowed in the house. That's why the cat lived in the garage. It had a basket, a box and was fed there. Thornbush did take good care of his cat. The animal was very much attached to him. When Mrs. Thornbush conceived the plan to deliver the corpse of her husband to Sandra Bent, she dragged the body to the garage where the blue Simca had been parked all this time. She took the suitcases from the hall and coolly counted out exactly one fourth of the loot. When she arrived in the garage with the money, she received the shock of her life. The black tomcat was seated on the chest of her dead husband and howled its sorrow for all to hear."

"Rather strange," sighed Vledder, "one expects it from dogs, somehow. But it explains the cat's fur on his clothes."

DeKok nodded slowly.

"Yes, the poor dumb brute was the only one to mourn his passing."

About the Author:

Albert Cornelis Baantjer (BAANTJER) is the most widely read author in the Netherlands. In a country with less than 15 million inhabitants, almost one out of every four people has bought a Baantjer book. More than 40 titles in his "DeKok" series have been written and almost 4 million copies have been sold. Baantjer can safely be considered a publishing phenomenon. In addition he has written other fiction and non-fiction and writes a daily column for a Dutch newspaper. It is for his "DeKok" books, however, that he is best known. *Every* year more than 700,000 Dutch people check a "Baantjer/DeKok" out of a library. The Dutch version of the Reader's Digest Condensed Books (called "Best Books" in Holland) has selected a Baantjer/DeKok book seven (7) times for inclusion in its series of condensed books.

Baantjer writes about Detective-Inspector DeKok of the Amsterdam Municipal Police (Homicide). Baantjer is himself a former inspector of the Amsterdam Police and is able to give his fictional characters the depth and the personality of real characters encountered during his long (38 years) police career. Many people in Holland sometimes confuse real-life Baantjer with fictional DeKok. The careful, authorized translations of his work published by InterContinental Publishing should fascinate the English speaking world as it has the Dutch reading public.